Elaytay (Tay)'s Adventures in Space and Time

Part Two

"We Meet At Last"

by

Lauresa Tomlinson

Young of Heart Publishing

McKinleyville, CA   95519

Table of Contents

WE MEET AT LAST

Chapter One
Back For a Visit

It had been a little over thirteen sectos (years) since we had been to earth. And now we were on our way back. We had first left when Elmosa (Wolf) was real small and now, Elmosa (Wolf) was finally going to have a chance to see his birth planet again.

"We are now free of the planet's gravitational pull, Captain," announced Paleeto (Pal).

Paleeto (Pal) is an old friend and had been with me on the ship that brought my family and me back to my home planet. But Captain Norzalon (Red) is new to our team. He is a space explorer that had come to our planet as an exchange pilot. He is the best-trained pilot we could get to fly the new ship. His people, the Norz-men, already have a colony on Earth, so that is the other reason for him going to Earth with us. It was a little hard at first getting used to seeing a humanoid with fire red hair and dark eyes. But he seems to know what he is doing and seems to be an even handed person.

Everyone is settling back into the regular space travel routines. Right now all we really have to do is watch for space debris and listen for incoming messages.

Mozla (Jeff), Rogna (Rodger) and Elmosa (Wolf) have brought their schoolwork and games to keep themselves busy. Just in case there wasn't enough information in the ship's computer systems about Earth to keep them busy.

"This is real interesting, Mozla (Jeff). Hey, Rogna (Rodger) have you had a chance to see this article copied from the networks of Palids?" asked Elmosa (Wolf).

"No I haven't, not yet, hang on a keptrons (minute). I want to see It," came Rogna (Rodger)'s answer.

"Earth has plants that when touched can make a person's skin itch and blister," said Elmosa (Wolf).

"I want to see that one, leave that program on till I can get over there," said Rogna (Rodger).

"There are even pictures of the plants that have this acid," added Mozla (Jeff).

As the boys did their work and check the computer logs, they found even more information on Earth and its animals, plant life and peoples.

A few pestrons (weeks) had gone by and so far everything was running smoothly. We were well on our way when one of the panels caught fire. All of a sudden I felt myself stricken with fear. I felt as if I was frozen in place.

My thoughts were racing. *'What do I do? I'm only the communications officer and this is a new ship that I know very little about. I had to fight with a conscious effort to slow my breathing. I must be calm, my actions will be noticed. I have to calm my breathing, in slow..., very slow..., hold..., now out very...slow, now again, and again. Ok, that's better.'* As I came back to what was going on around me, I found that it was just a miner fire and that Paleeto (Pal) had extinguished it quickly.

I looked at Paleeto (Pal), he smiled and said. *"What you just went through will be our little secret. No one else heard you I'm sure... they were all busy for a few moments."*

"I'm sorry for panicking, it's just that the last crash I was in started just like that, and I guess I still haven't gotten over the fright I felt from being the only survivor on a New World," I said.

"Sometimes it takes a while to get over experiences like the one you had and it is sometimes

even harder to keep your thoughts centered,"
Paleeto (Pal) assured.

*"I was a first sectos (year) cadet when I had
to learn to center the hard way. I too was on a ship
that went down. I was knocked out and when I came
to, I found myself underwater. If I hadn't learned a
few centering techniques I may have drowned that
sestron (day),"* Paleeto (Pal) added.

*"Maybe, that if and when the time allowed
it may be, I too, could learn a new way to center. At
this point the only method I know is by slowing the
breath,"* I looked at him and with a smile said.
*"Maybe one of these days when we have time you
can teach me your way."*

*"It is very simple, I use sound. I hold a
special tone in my head. You may have to ask your
higher source for your tone, because not everyone
has the same tone,"* Paleeto (Pal) said simply.

*"You have some time now, if you want to go
try out different sounds. But you have to know that
different sounds do different things to each group of
peoples."* he continued.

"I'm not following." I questioned.

*"Well, one tone may put my race in a
peaceful frame of mind while that same tone may
make another group of peoples think quicker. Some
tones can help build the body, mind and spirit of a
group, while other tones generate too much energy
for the body to take care of,"* he explained.

*"Ok...I think I understand...So what you're
saying is that there is a tone for my race that will
help us think clearly and another for getting us to*

explore and invent. But at the same time there are tones that will make us angry and irritable, right?" I asked.

"Yes, you have it. But I'm not sure how much tone or sound has been studied on your home planet. Some planets haven't studied the effects that sounds have on the body and thought processes. For instance you know that when Elmosa (Wolf) was young that certain songs would help him sleep while other song would make him want to play." Paleeto (Pal) said as he looked at me.

I nodded my head and smiled. *"Yes, there were."* I said

"Well, my group of people have found that certain tones work real good for one group and yet when we use that same tone on a person from a mixed parent background, this person sometimes needed to be counted as a new group. And so a different tone is needed, and again sometimes there are several planets that can use most of the same tones with just a few minor changes. I think that it may have something to do with the vibratory rate of the planet they are from or have spent most of their lives on." he explained.

"All of this is very interesting to me. Do you have time to tell me more about sound and the studies from your planet?" I asked.

"I'll have to check on a few things, but while I am doing that, we have some information about sound and its effects on things in our compulink (computer). Check under vibratory wave studies." he said.

As I checked the compulink information
I found that our beaming methods in the
beginning used light waves. I also found that
some peoples couldn't see the transporter beam
that was being used and so a light of a lower
vibration was added to the transporter beam so
it could be seen. But at the same time the teller
(light) could be taken out of the transporter
beam so that transport could be done without
anyone knowing, (unless they were there and
watching the person or object disappear). I also
found that sounds are very useful in the
healing of the physical, mental, spiritual and
emotional bodies of all creations and that some
sounds are harmful while other sounds helped.
I counted myself lucky at that point in my
study, that I had never been subjected to
harmful sounds that I knew of. Some sounds or
vibrations, heard and unheard, can cause
illness and sometimes even death of some
beings. Vibrations from unheard sounds all the
way through the wave length including unseen
colors can be used in very many ways to help
and harm living things. Every created thing has
a vibratory rate.

"So was this information okay?" asked
Paleeto (Pal).

*"I guess it will have to do for now unless
you have found something more."* I said, hoping
he would say yes.

"No this is all that is available for right now. But I did get through to my world and gained permission for you to study it in more detail, there, when you get back and you are ready." Paleeto (Pal) explained.

Chapter Two
Sasquatch or Yeti?

'If anything, all this information was very interesting and I could see where the knowledge would come in real handy. I also know that the study of the vibratory rates of sound through light was far from being finished. I would love to get back to a creation dome and do even more studies of it, but that would have to wait, and for now I would have to deal with the information I was given.' I was shaken from my deep thoughts.....

"Mom, Mom, did you know that there are other intelligent life forms on the planet earth other than the people we know about." Elmosa (Wolf) said excitedly.

"Ok... so what have you found that you think may be another form of intelligent life?" I ask. I had been taught from a very early age that each time you tell of the things you have learned or go over something you are learning, that you are teaching yourself at the same time.

"Come and take a look at what I've found in the compulink banks." he said pointing at a videe (movie) that was playing on the holographic grid.

"So what references does it give to this being on earth?" I ask.

"This compulink bank says these people were called the bear people of Onaska in the Beneefer system and that an exploration party was left on Earth a long time ago, back when the earth was still in a state of confusion with a lot if volcanic activity. Do you think there still may be some of these people on the planet?" he asked.

Strong Bow walked up about that time and looked at the hologram of this bear person that we had been looking at.

"Ah... Sasquatch" said Strong Bow.

"Who?" asked Elmosa (Wolf).

"Sasquatch" repeated Strong Bow looking at Elmosa (Wolf) with a grin on his face.

Seeing the confused look on Elmosa (Wolf)'s face, he knew that this was an area that would have been good to cover in the creation domes while they had the chance. But at this point he would just have to explain the best he could who these furry people were.

"Sasquatch... that is what my people call them. They are called by many names including the bear people. We have never been harmed by one of their people and they have always been kind to us. When one of our small children have gotten lost and we can't find them before dark, one of the Sasquatch would bring them back when they were able find them. In payment we would give them food and things we thought they would like to have. They are a very simple people and they want very little. Because they don't mingle with most of the people on the planet they have been able to keep their race pure, of loose thinking and unneeded clutter." he explained.

"Tell me more, dad." Elmosa (Wolf) pleaded.

"Ok, well they are very tall, about seven and a half to nine lifnas (feet) tall. They seem to look like a cross between the bear and humans, and the females in most cases seem to be darker than the males. They bury their dead like we do, and they honor the Great Creator as we do. They care very much for the Earth and their young and eat mostly fruits and vegetables. I'm not sure where they live. Although I have heard that some live in caves while other groups roam the lands. They take such good care of the land that it is rare that you will know when they have been in the area except for an odor." Strong Bow explained with the hint of a chuckle.

"An odor? Elmosa (Wolf) asked.

"Yes, sometime they stink more than they do at other times. I think it may have something to do with their diets." said Strong Bow.

"Do you think that Grandfather can help me find one? I would really like to meet a Sasquatch." ask Elmosa (Wolf).

"I really don't know if Grandfather will know how to get in touch with them, but we can ask him when we get there. But not right away. We will be on the planet for at least one full turn of the moon." Strong Bow said.

"I'm glad we will be there at least that long, because there seems to be a lot of things to do and see on planet Earth." said Elmosa (Wolf).

"That is true. There are quite a few things I want to show all of you. I think you will be pleased with what you experience there." said Strong Bow.

Captain Norzalon (Red) walked into the area about that time. The hologram of Sasquatch was still standing in front of

us. "Ah, a Yeti." he said. "A what? Elmosa
(Wolf) said with all of us looking at him.
        "A Yeti that is what my people call
this being. The ones I have heard stories of
are about nine lifnas (feet) tall and have
white fur all over their bodies. My people
have seen lots of them in the heavy snow
areas. We don't know what they eat or
where they live. They must know things
that we haven't dreamed of yet though,
because they seem to multiply. They only
hurt one person in our group and he was a
renegade that didn't care about the Earth or
anything except making a profit. Even at
that, him getting hurt was his own doing.
They wrecked some machines he was using
to tear up the Earth and he happened to be
in one of them. He went out in the ice land
and made messes everywhere he went and
tore up the Earth and left animal parts all
over the open ground. Well I guess they
didn't like that. The next time we saw him,
he was laying on his sled right outside
camp, dead and all of his trash and animal
parts laying on the ground all around him.
But they seem to help those who are really
in need of help. They have helped save a
number of my people during storms."
Norzalon (Red) explained.

"We are three keptrons (30 min.) from entering the gravitational pull of Earth." Shouted Paleeto (Pal).

"Everyone in their places. Elaytay (Tay) send a message back to base and tell them we are getting ready to land on Earth." ordered Norzalon (Red).

"Message sent, reply coming in from Marsla relay. Message reads as follows sir, "Keep complete records of all experiences and experiments, reports due after each lift off. Signed: Nenapol (Paul) Commander of Marsla relay station." I said.

"Good, I will drop all of you off, the will go to check in on my people's colony. I will report on them on my way back to pick all of you up. Then you will put in your reports as we lift off on our way back to Cyterrious." said Captain Norzalon (Red).

"Yes sir, the reports will be ready in the time needed." I said.

"Everyone buckle in, we are going in for a landing." said Paleeto (Pal).

"How close are we going to be where I crashed the first time?" I asked.

"Well, let me put it this way, Strong Bow's people have moved their camp a little farther upstream and we will be landing in a glen on the lower side of the falls near their camp." said Paleeto (Pal).

"Oh, that sounds real good." I said.

"Do we have sound systems on the outside of this ship?" asked Strong Bow.

"Yes, Why?" asked Paleeto (Pal).

"I have my flute with me and I thought it might be nice to let them know who we were before we landed. I still remember a few of the family's favorite tunes." Strong Bow said.

"Oh, well in that case, have fun." Paleeto (Pal) said as he flipped a switch.

Strong Bow began to play one of the most pleasing melodies I hadn't heard in a long time. At that point we were close enough to the landing site that Paleeto (Pal) opened the wide angle view port, so we could all see what was going on outside. From where we were landing we could see the camp. The younger children were lining up on the other side of the stream, laughing and jumping up and down. Then I could make out Heal Waters and Papa Two Wolves making their way to the edge of the stream. Healing Waters started to wade out into the water. We had landed now and could all take the safety belts off and get to the doors.

Chapter Three
Unwanted Visitors

As the doors opened Healing Waters was standing waiting at the base of the ramp. And as the ramp made its final move I was standing at the top ready to go down it.

"White Dove, Elaytay (Tay), we have been waiting for all of you and the rest of our family and friends to come back." Healing Waters said as she gave me a hug and her eyes searched the doorway for the rest of the group.

As I gave Healing Waters a hug, Papa Two Wolves walked up beside her and proceeded to give a group hug to Healing Waters and me.

"My family is finally united again. I've been waiting for this for a long time. Your mother and I have sat many a night watching the night sky, wondered how you, Strong Bow and Singing Wolf (Elmosa (Wolf)) were doing." said Papa Two Wolves.

"I too have wondered many of times how you and mom were doing." I said giving them both another hug.

About that time Strong Bow came down the ramp, arms packed with some of the things we had brought back with us.

"Strong Bow, I am very glad to see you are well." said Papa Two Wolves.

I took some of the things from Strong Bow's arms so he was able to give both Healing Waters and Two Wolves hugs.

"Yes, I am fine and our son has grown very strong and tall." said Strong Bow.

At that point Elmosa (Wolf), Mozla (Jeff) and Rogna (Rodger) all showed up in the doorway holding bundles. Two Wolves looked up and saw the boys. He seemed to know right off, which one of the boys was Singing Wolf.

"Elmosa (Wolf), this is Two Wolves and Healing Waters, your Grandparents. They are the healers of the tribe." said Strong Bow, smiling and looking at all of us.

Elmosa (Wolf) put down the bundles he was holding and gave his Grandparents a big group hug.

"Singing Wolf, you are almost a man. While you are here I will help get you ready for the changing test. When you past this test, then you have all of the rights of a man here in our tribe." said Two Wolves.

"I think you will be pleasantly surprised to find that he and his friends has been instructed very well." said Strong Bow. "This is Mozla (Jeff) and Rogna (Rodger) two of Elmosa (Wolf)'s best friends." he continued.

"Singing Wolf?" Mozla (Jeff) questioned.

"Yes, this was the name that was given to Elmosa (Wolf) when he was born. Elaytay (Tay) thought since we were going back to her home planet that he would need a name more suitable for that planet so he could fit in. So his whole name is, Elmosa (Wolf) Singing Wolf of the People of the Sun." said Two Wolves proudly.

"Do you have to be born here on this planet in order to get a name from the tribe?" ask Mozla (Jeff) and Rogna (Rodger) almost together.

"No, but due to the fact that you were born somewhere else like Elaytay (Tay), you will have to be given the name by the tribe and it may even have to be earned." said Two Wolves.

"*Paleeto (Pal)!, old friend.*" said Healing Waters as Paleeto (Pal) came to the doorway to look out.

"Ah, Healing Waters." he said out loud and gave a bow. Then in silence, "*How have you been? And how are things with the rest of your people?"*

Healing Waters began to laugh, "We have had some troubles but in so many sectos (years) all has gone pretty well. And I can still hear you. Thank you for asking." she said. "Are you going to be staying with us for a while?" she continued.

"No, not at this time, I have duties on the other side of your planet with our new captain. But I have been learning to talk out loud" he said.

"So is this all of our visitors?" Two Wolves said looking around at all of us with a smiling and a chuckle, then he motioned for us to follow him back to the camp.

"Elaytay (Tay), do you have everything you are going to need?" ask Paleeto (Pal).

I looked around at all of the bundles that Strong Bow and the boys had carried from the ship. "Yes, I think so, except for my log recorder and all the plants we brought to be planted." I said.

Paleeto (Pal) pulled the recorder out from behind his back with a grin. "I thought you may be needing this and we will leave the plants here before we take off." he said. "Okay, well, we will be back in one full turn of the moon and we will land right here. Oh,

and I included a list of items Norzalon (Red)
is needing too." he continued.

He waved, smiled and went back
inside, as we left with Healing Waters and
Papa Two Wolves.

We had just crossed the stream when
they lifted off. I looked where we had landed
and sure enough there were the plants, all
neatly stacked.

"So how is Meninso (Mens) doing?"
asked Healing Waters.

"Just fine, he was transferred to
Okanis, another planet to do further studies
on the Lanapukas." I said.

"A Lana what?" asked Two Wolves.

"Lanapukas, a type of large bird." I
said.

"Oh." came the reply from both of
them.

I smiled and we all walked on into
camp. "Where is Running Bear?" asked
Strong Bow looking at Two Wolves.

"Running Bear is your other
grandfather." I said looking at Elmosa (Wolf).

He nodded at me as we continued
walking.

A figure ran toward us from across the
camp, waving her hands and laughing. As
the figure came closer, you could make out
her face.

"That's...Morning Star from the creation dome." said the boys, sounding like a chorus.

"Yes, yes it is matter of fact." Strong Bow said with a large smile. "Elmosa (Wolf), I want you to meet your aunt." he continued.

"You're my dad's sister?" Elmosa (Wolf) asked, looking at Morning Star, which was standing in front of them now, almost out of breath, but smiling brightly.

"Yes." she answered. "I am, and all of you are looking at me strangely." she continued.

"Oh, well, that is a long story. I will try to explain all of it to you later." said Strong Bow. "Where is Dad? I haven't seen him yet. Is he ok?" he asked showing concern.

"Well, I think he ate something that didn't agree with him. He hasn't felt well for a few days." she said.

"Well then, I think that Running Bear should be our first stop." I said.

As we continued across the camp we could hear whispers coming from the boys as they trailed us. I knew most that they were talking about Morning Star. I knew what Strong Bow had done in the creation domes but they didn't know I knew. So it was sort of funny hearing all this excited whispering going on between them.

Morning Star turned and smiled at the boys a couple of times.

"Come on boys, your lagging behind." I said.

"Ok, we're coming." said Elmosa (Wolf) as they stepped up the pace.

"I'm telling you it's the same girl." said Mozla (Jeff), trying to whisper even lower, so not to be heard.

"Well, I'm still not sure if it is or not. There is a little difference between the two. But so far I think I like this one a little better." said Rogna (Rodger).

"I still say that Dad's little sister was the Morning Star that he put in the creation dome along with Healing Waters and Two Wolves and the rest of the tribe. It has to have been the area and all of the people are two close to the one that were in the creation dome programs." said Elmosa (Wolf).

"Well, I guess we can ask later to night after the rest of the people go to bed. Can't we?" interjected Rogna (Rodger).

"That's true, but for now if we don't catch up closer to the rest of the party, we may get into trouble." said Elmosa (Wolf).

"Here is where you and Elaytay (Tay) will be sleeping tonight." said Two Wolves.

"And in that place is where the boys will be." added Healing Waters pointing to a half made lean-to.

"The rest of the young men in training can sleep near the edge of the camp with teachers." Papa Two Wolves added.

We put all of the things we brought with us in our dwelling except for the medical gear. "We had better go see how Running Bear is and what we may have to do to help get him on his feet again." I said.

"Yes, show me to my Father's dwelling." said Strong Bow.

"Follow me." said Healing Water, motioning to us to follow her.

Morning Star ran ahead of us like a deer. Running and jumping.

"She is one of the fastest runners we have in the tribe. She is also a good mud walker." said Healing Waters with pride in her voice.

Strong Bow took a long breath with a look of pride too and for good reason, this was his little sister that Healing Waters was bragging about.

"But of course you weren't slow either when you where her age." said Healing Water looking over at Strong Bow. Morning Star had reached Running Bear's dwelling and went in to sit with him. As we came closer, she stuck her head out the door.

"He is breathing a little easier now than what he was earlier today." she said.

"That's good." I said, as we all walked past her into the dwelling.

"Hi Father, How are you feeling?" asked Strong Bow.

"Better now that you're home again. I think I ate something that made me sick." said Running Bear.

"Well, lay back and let us take a look at you. I want to run a few test on you and see if we can make sure what it is that is making you sick." I said. "I'm going to have to stick you with this needle, and I'm going to leave it in place. So I want you to hold very still for a while. Ok? Don't move. You can talk, but don't move any other part of your body. OK?" I continued.

Chapter Four
Minus X men

"Ok, like you said, I won't move." he said.

We went on with testing. After a few keptrons (minutes) I found what I thought may point to a problem. I knew by the last test I had run, that it wasn't something that Running Bear had eaten, that was making him sick.

I looked over at Strong Bow, as our eyes met, "You may have to do a physical search for the cause. I will explain to you what you may be searching for. But I have one more test to run before I will know for sure." I said.

"What are you thinking it may be?" asked Strong Bow.

"I think it may be a possible implant by a group of beings I will call minus X." I said.

"The who?" Strong Bow asked.

"Minus X are an astral (fourth dimensional) race of short, gray skinned beings with large heads and black eyes that have

found a way to slow down their vibration rate
to work in the third dimension for a short
time.. They have lost all feelings and emotions
due to playing God (Creator) with their own
genetics. Now they have problems. They
played with the genes that governed feelings
and emotions until they retarded them too far.
Now their race can't feel nor have emotions. On
their planet the pollution was very high and it
played havoc with their feelings and emotions
so in order to keep their feelings and emotions
in control, they kept retarding them till now
they don't have them at all. So now they go to
unaware planets and place implants into the
people of that planet to transmit back the
feelings and emotions of the one they have
place implants in. The transmitions they
receive let them feel the emotions of their
victims and it is like a drug to them and they
are hooked. At any rate there are certain signs
that show up if one of the devices have been
put into a humanoid body. Sometimes it makes
them sick like a bad case of the flu or a real bad
head cold or stomachaches or pain in one area
of the body. I can test for unnatural Neuronic
Electrical Impulses in the body. At that point
we will have to do a visual of that part of the
body. Sometimes the cut or puncture will be
real small, as small as a sixteenth of an lanfa
(inch) in the skin. But I have found them in the
soft tissue, where they had been put internally

through a natural opening in the body." I explained.

"Ok, I have the reading on the N.E.I. test and there seems to be a problem in the mid abdominal region, the solar plexus area." I said.

"Oh, yes, I think I have found something." said Strong Bow.

"Show me the place you are talking about." I said as I turned around from putting away the testing equipment and grabber my bright luma and a magnifier to help me see it better..

"Yes I think you may have found the spot." I said.

"Running Bear, How long have you had this cut?" I ask pointing at the small-healed cut just above his belly button.

"I don't know, I don't think it was there the other day, before I got sick." he said, looking at the spot with a confused look on his face.

"Tell me the story of what has happened to you, starting the day before you got sick and started having pain while I remove the transmitter." I said.

"Well, it was day before yesterday, I got up to go hunting with some of the others men. Everything was going real good. Then a deer I shot jumped over a small cliff, I went down after the deer while the rest of the men tracked some of the smaller game in the area. I went down to the base and was dressing the deer when the sun light got real bright and I couldn't see anything. It got real hot and I couldn't move, then I heard what I thought were voices talking. I managed to look around and saw these small type people I think, they were more like silhouettes. One of them poked me in that spot with something sharp. Then the next thing I know I was laying on the ground next to the deer and Tall Grass was bent over me." he said.

"Well, I am going to scan the area with sound and see exactly where the thing is that was put inside of you. If it is like most it will have shifted a little from where it was first placed. Ok?" I asked.

"Yes, do that, I don't like feeling like this, it hurts bad." he said.

"Strong Bow, hand me the marker from the case." I said pointing to a case just out of reach.

"This one?" he asked.

"Yes, good, I think I have found the implant. It's right.... here." I said, as I made a dot on Running Bear's abdomen.

"I am going to make a small cut right where the dot is and take out the implant that was put in. Ok?" I asked. "But first I will rub in a liquid so the cut won't hurt." I added.

"Good, just do it. Take this thing out." he said.

"Good, done, it's out. See, this small thing, this was what was causing all that pain." I said, holding up a very small odd shaped chip.

"All that pain was coming from this?" Running Bear said as he reaches out for the chip and sat up.

"Well, how do you feel now?" asked Strong Bow.

"Good, real good, I have a real need to go see how the rest of the men are that where in the area at the time." he said, as he went out the door.

"Tall Grass, call a meeting of the people." Running Bear said.

Tall Grass nodded and went through the village gathering the people.

When everyone was together, Running Bear related the story of what had happened to him in the forest, and then asked if anything else like that had happened to anyone in the rest of the tribe.

Running Elk and Sister Wolf both had stories to tell about these beings. It seemed that Running Elk was one of the men on the hunt the day that Running Bear was taken. He too had been hit with the hot sunbeam. He was being pulled from the earth when a large Sasquatch jumped into the beam and let out one of the most savage screams he had ever heard and the beam stopped and they were both dropped to the ground. Running Elk said he felt a little weak after the drop and the Sasquatch stayed with him till the other men started coming.

"I think these beings are frightened of our brothers, the Sasquatch." said Running Elk, with a grin on his face.

"It would seem so." said Sister Wolf. "I too was helped by our big friends. I was out gathering herbs for our evening meal when I was caught in the sun beam, and I was grabbed out of the hot beam by one of our big friends." she continued.

Chapter Five
Space Plants and Zigmo

"So is everyone else alright?" I asked, looking around.

Everyone smiled and looked at each other, so I took it at that, that everyone else was ok.

Grandmother Hawk came into the center of the circle.

"It is time for celebration...Running Bear is feeling better again and everyone is full of joy and thanks giving." she said.

"Mom, does that mean that it is time to eat?" Elmosa (Wolf) asked

"Yes it does." Strong Bow said, answering for me with a large smile, and putting his hand on Elmosa (Wolf)'s shoulder.

I walked closer to where the three boys were.

"Rogna (Rodger), have you boys taken care of the plants and seedlings we brought with us." I ask looking at all three of them.

"No not yet, but we will do that now."
said Rogna (Rodger) with Mozla (Jeff)
nodding.

All three of the boys took off running
across the meadow to where we had left the
plants, seedlings, the presents and the rest of
the supplies earlier in the day.

"Well it looks like this trip will be a
good one, Love." Strong Bow said putting his
arms around me.

I smiled and nodded. This was a
peaceful moment and felt real good.

The drumming was starting and the
fire was reaching for the sky. Everyone was
joining in the celebration of the day. Tonight
was to be a night of singing, dancing, eating
and having fun.

We all celebrated late into the night
then went to sleep with peaceful thoughts and
good dreams. But needless to say amacron
(morning) came early and there was plenty of
work to be done.

Elmosa (Wolf), Rogna (Rodger) and
Mozla (Jeff) finished their lean-to by hanging
up a blanket over the opening. They were
greeted early by the rest of the boys in camp,
who had great things planned for the day.
Elmosa (Wolf), Rogna (Rodger) and Mozla
(Jeff) were each handed bows and were asked
to come join in the games of the day.

They didn't know it but they were going to be shown the ways of the tribe, then tested later on what they had learned. Rogna (Rodger), Mozla (Jeff) and Elmosa (Wolf) were already pretty good at most of the games. They had been taught most of them in the Creation Dome of the planet they had all called home in the past sectos (years). The teachers of the tribe helped the children learn through games and contests. Later in the evening they would sitting and listen to the stories of the people. This was their history time, the stories were put in memory so they too could tell them to the younger children while an elder listened to make sure it was told right and nothing was left out. This was how they all knew who they were and where their people came from. Elmosa (Wolf) was to soon find out that he was a part of that history, and that he was making history in everything he did and said. That was a lot of pressure but Strong Bow and I thought he was strong enough to handle it.

Strong Bow and I picked up the plants and seedling we had brought and carried them over to the garden area that Healing Water and some of the others were working in.

I put the seedlings that I had been carrying, down next to Healing Waters.

"These are some of the plants and seedling that we brought with us." I said pointing to the seedlings and the plants that Strong Bow was still holding.

Healing Waters looked up from her work in the garden.

"These plants are different from any I have ever seen." she said, standing to look more closely at the plants.

"Yes these are plants that we have found work best for some of the more common illnesses of earth. I talked the counsel into letting me bring these plants and seedlings with us. This way you will have the herbs needed for some of the ills that may happen in the future. I have all of the written information on these plants...I even have it written in your language so others can read it. This way I thought would be better and you can pass the information on to others." I said.

"I am glad you have brought these to us." said Healing Waters.

"I have memorized all of the information on these plants and seedlings...if you want I can relate that information to you first hand." Strong Bow said, then looked over at me and smiled.

I nodded and smiled back. He knew something I didn't but I knew he would tell me later when the time came.

"I have other things to check on, so I will be back a little later." I said.

Both Healing Waters and Strong Bow smiled and nodded.

I really needed to get back to the tent to check on one of the pets I brought with me. No one knew that I had brought Zigmo with me. He was a strange looking little creature. Sort of like a small flat faced cat with round ears and a tail that curled into a set of circles. Zigmo didn't walk like a normal four-legged animal, he jumped like a big bullfrog. He had short orange fur all over his body except on his head, where it was longer like a lion's mane with brown stripe mixed with the orange. He also had white tufts of fur protruding out of his ears. Zigmo's eyes were very large, set closely together and almost sky blue. He seemed to be able to hear and see everything around him. I don't think anything could sneak up on Zigmo.

As I was sitting and playing with Zigmo, Elmosa (Wolf) pulled up the door of the dwelling and came in. Zigmo's head turns all the way around to see in back of him, like that of an owl.

"What is that Mom?" Elmosa (Wolf) asked in surprise.

"Oh, this is Zigmo, he's a pet I brought from our home planets." I said with a chuckle.

"Planets?" Elmosa (Wolf) questioned.

"Yes, Earth and Cyterrious. Zigmo is a cross, a mix up in the DNA sample I gathered over thirteen sectos (years) ago when I was here. When Enah 2 (E 2) was working with the DNA samples Zigmo's parents were brought into creation. Believe me they were just as funny looking as Zigmo. His kind only lives about ten sectos (years) and Zigmo is about five now." I explained.

"Go ahead, you can pet him, he loves people. Zig only eats plants and insects, nothing larger than his paw." I continued.

"Why did you bring Zigmo to earth with us?" asked Elmosa (Wolf).

"Well, I had a couple of reasons, number one, I couldn't find anyone that had the time to take care of him while we were on this mission and number two, I sort of wanted to see what the slight changes in pressures would do to him. I brought a cage, he has been raised in one. He is only use to being out of a cage only a little while at a time." I said.

"Sometimes I think you take too many chances in the name of science, Mom." said Elmosa (Wolf).

"I really didn't want to leave him behind or have him put down just because we were going on this mission. Besides I thought that our family on this planet would like to see a strange animal. Don't you." I asked, while playing with Zigmo.

"I think they might have a lot of fun seeing something strange. And he is really strange." said Elmosa (Wolf), looking at him very closely.

Zigmo protruded his long tongue out in a licking motion and moved it across Elmosa (Wolf)'s chin and cheek.

"Uck, oooooo." Elmosa (Wolf) said as he backed away.

I had to laugh, I didn't know that Zigmo's tongue was that long. He licked Elmosa (Wolf) in the nose.

"Uck, it's not that funny Mom." he said.

"I can't help it, the look on your face just did it. It was so funny." I said, still laughing.

Zigmo leaned back and you would have thought he was very proud of himself the way he looked. He tried speaking at that point. His voice was real low and rough, almost what one would call gravelly. Zigmo didn't sound quiet like a cat. I wasn't sure what he sounded like. He would alter his voice like as if he was trying to learn to talk. Some time it sounded like he said hello. Zigmo was an incredible animal.

"Well, I have to put him away for right now, so I can get back to helping with the garden. Oh, Yes and what did you want when you first came in?" I asked.

"I was just going to get my round'o, I wanted to show the boys that I had a toy. And that when I let go of it and it gets to the end of its string, it would come back up to me." he said.

"I'll see you later Mom." he said as he went out the door.

I finished putting Zigmo back in his cage and went back to the garden.

"Hi, how is it going?" I ask as I walked up.

"So far so good." Strong Bow said.

Healing Waters looked up putting her hand above of her eyes so she could see me.

"Some of these plants have odd root systems." she said. holding up one.

"The roots seem to go in all directions at the same time." she continued.

"Yes, I see what you mean. Those are the plants that need to be planted in mounds a few feet away from the others. If you plant them close together, they will die in a short time." I explained.

"Yes, I understand, Strong Bow told me all that. I just think they look really weird." she said with a smile.

"Well I have to agree with you on that fact." I said.

"We have most of the larger plants planted, so all we have to do now is take care of the seedlings." said Strong Bow.

"Ok, it looks like I got back just in time.
I brought a few things that will help with the
seedlings. There are trays and nutrients,
which we can make more of later from things
that are already on this planet. I will show you
different things you have on earth to combine
that will help the plants grow strong." I said.
"There are a few things that you can put in the
ground with the seeds and young plants that
will help them grow faster and stronger." I
continued.

Rogna (Rodger) came walking up
about that time, carrying a flute he had just
finished making.

"Rogna (Rodger) are you through with
your studies for today?" I asked.

"Yes, I learned a lot of things today
about life on this planet. And look what I
made, Running Bear said that Elmosa (Wolf)
and I were the fastest students he has in wood
work." he said, with a big smile.

"What about Mozla (Jeff)?" I asked.

"Oh, he's real good about remembering
the stories and learning the tracks of animals.
Running Bear said Mozla (Jeff) would be a
good hunter." he said. "What are all of you
doing?" he continued.

"We are getting the soil ready to put in
the seedlings. Do you want to help?" I asked.

"Sure, what do I do?" he asked.

"Well, you can go with me to gather the soil under the dead plants, and what is under that log over there." said Strong Bow.

"Make sure you don't gather any of the soil around the base of an evergreen tree." I reminded him

"An evergreen tree?" Rogna (Rodger) asked.

"Yes, the ones that looks like that one." I said pointing to a pine tree. "If they don't have regular type leaves like, say the dogwood or maple over there," I said pointing to some other trees nearby. "it is usually hard to grow things in the soil from under the evergreen trees. Strong Bow knows what to look for, he will show you." I continued.

"Yes, I know what she means and I will show you how to tell the difference, and what to look for." Strong Bow said.

Chapter Six
Saving Notnah (Not)

Healing Waters and I started to make the rows for the seedlings and left the middles of each row needing soil. This way when Rogna (Rodger) and Strong Bow came back we could fill the middles of the rows with the soil they brought back and then plant the seedlings.

It was late afternoon when they came back with baskets of soil.

"Good, we are ready for the soil to be put in the centers of each of these rows." I said pointing at the rows we had made.

"That looks easy enough." said Rogna (Rodger).

Soon all of the seedlings were in the ground and we were getting really hungry.

The children came running past us heading for the center of the camp.

"What's all of the hurry?" Rogna (Rodger) yelled at one of the children.

"It's time to eat!" one yelled back while running past.

"Oh, Good. I thought I was going to go hungry." said Strong Bow.

"No, not a chance. Someone in the camp will always cook the meal when the rest of us are at work, that the good part of living as one large family. Now if someone in your direct family say like Mozla (Jeff), because he is under you care, was to come down sick, then you would be excused from your normal duties to the tribe. But your new job would be to take care of the ill ones and help with the meals for the rest of the camp. Unless you and the council thought it better if someone else cared for the ill ones." said Healing Waters.

"I have always liked that rule, it seemed like a good one. That way everything seems to run real smooth for our people." said Strong Bow.

"Come let's go eat. Tomorrow I will take you to meet Singing Sun and his people." said Two Wolves, who had been standing nearby.

"Oh good, I haven't seen them since I was very young," said Strong Bow.

After dinner we all turned in so we could get up early the next amacron (morning). The way to Singing Sun's camp was east by about half a day's journey from ours.

In my dreams I would often dream of coming back to earth, but now I found that I was dreaming of my own birth planet. I guess it is the minds way of keeping us from missing what we don't have at the time. Everyone was settled down and almost asleep but I couldn't seem to keep my eyes closed. It seemed it was going to be one of those nights that I would just catch bits of sleep here and there.

"AAAAYAH...Owoooooo...Kaaaaack!"

"What is that?" I said sitting up straight.

"That sounds like a Sasquatch in trouble. We have to go see, now." said Strong Bow.

We went outside and there we met Healing Waters, Two Wolves and Running Bear. "It seems that the sound is coming from that way." said Running Bear pointing.

Yes, I think your right." said Two Wolves, holding a pouch of herbs and leather strips.

I ducked back into the tent and grabbed me medical bag and CAK (ray gun) then ran to catch up with the others.

We could still hear the screams as we all walked very quickly through the forest. The light of the moon peeped in on the forest floor just enough to keep us from tripping.

When we got closer we could see that it was a young Sasquatch that had wondered off from the rest of its kind. It was being held in a light beam and clutching its arm. We could see that it had been hurt and needed help quickly.

In the beam we could see other being possibly from the Vasitar system. And I knew that the United Planets Alliance had not given them permission to even come close to this planet. Much less taking or examining life on it.

"We have to get him out of the light! Now!" said Running Bear.

"Yes, we must, but how?" asked Healing Waters.

"Well whatever we do we're going need more help than just us." said Two Wolves.

At that point Two Wolves let out a screaming type yell and in a matter of moments two more Sasquatch came running.

"That scream is their way of asking for help. It seems that the little one is from another area and their screams are a little different." said Healing Waters.

The Sasquatch both looked at us and headed toward the light in a mad run. The larger of the two knocked the little one out of the beam and the other took out the gray being next to him.

As the Sasquatch held down the being, the light vanished and we could get to the little Sasquatch. They both took hold of the gray being, looked at all of us, then let out a high pitched squeal. The larger of the Sasquatch looked at Healing Waters then at the young Sasquatch and made a low rumbling sound and they took the being with them and left. It seems that with the act of trying to capture a Sasquatch these beings had started a small war with the Sasquatch. We helped the little one and he followed us back to camp.

Strong Bow saw that I was holding my CAK (ray gun) and asked, "Why didn't you shoot the bad guy in the beam?"

"If I had shot even the shortest beam it would have bounced around in the bean and may have hit the young one." I explained.

Next amacron (morning) came fast. When we all got up and checked on our new patient, we found he was doing real good. His arm had almost healed completely. Two Wolves offered him some fruit and bread.

"He is real young, I wonder what happened to his family?" said Healing Waters.

"I wonder if he was the last of his family to be taken?" I said.

"That could be the reason why the others took that being with them. Sort of like a hostage." said Strong Bow.

"Well, that could be. They acted like they knew what they were doing." said Running Bear.

"That makes me curious. I wonder if they have a way of communicating with other groups from other planets. Maybe they are a part of the Limited Federation of Planets." I said.

"I really don't know and we won't be able to find out until Norzalon (Red) comes back." said Strong Bow.

"Well what do we do with...what shall we call him?" ask Two Wolves.

"Notnah (Not) would be a good name. I mean after all he seems to be the last of his family, as far as we know. And besides when you ask, what we should call him, Notnah (Not) came to mind." said Mozla (Jeff)

"We agree" said Rogna (Rodger) and Elmosa (Wolf), who were all standing next to the young Sasquatch.

"I think that will make a good name for him." said Healing Waters.

We will call you Notnah (Not), ok?" Healing Waters asked, looking into the eyes of the young Sasquatch.

It was almost as if he smiled then he nodded in agreement.

"So who is going to stay with Notnah (Not) while we all go to Singing Sun's camp?" asked Elmosa (Wolf).

Everyone looked at each other.

"That might be a small problem. We can't just leave him here in the camp. Some of those beings may try to come and get him and that would cause even bigger problems." said Running Bear.

Chapter Seven
Sharing Stories

"Ok, we had better get moving if we plan of getting there in time." said Running Bear. "When we have walked down stream far enough, we will have to go over this hill, through the next valley and a little way into the next forest to be at Singing Sun's camp." he instructed..

Notnah (Not) stopped for water and picked some berries while Running Bear was telling us the way to Singing Sun's camp. I joined him in the picking of the berries.

"These are very good. Does anyone else want some?" I asked.

"We have time to take a small break and eat." said Two Wolves.

We all picked and ate berries and the bread we brought till we were full.

"Let's get going or it will be dark before we get to the camp." said Two Wolves.

As we walked and talked we could hear little sounds come from Notnah (Not) and the boys.

"Is everything ok back there with you boys?" I asked.

"Everything is going real good. Notnah (Not) has a very easy language or thought patterns to learn." said Rogna (Rodger).

"Yes Mom, we are learning a lot from him." said Elmosa (Wolf).

"Watch out Two Wolves! Duck!" yelled Healing Waters.

About that time a branch fell from the oak tree right in front of him. He ducked and the branch missed him. "Woe...that was close. How did you know that is was going to fall?" asked Two Wolves, looking back a Healing Waters.

He had been slightly ahead of Running Bear and Strong Bow was behind him. Healing Waters and I were just behind them and the boys were walking with Notnah (Not) just behind us. We were all walking on a deer path that lead nearby Singing Sun's camp.

"Notnah (Not) told me, and just in time too." she said.

"You mean you can hear what Notnah (Not) is saying too?" asked Elmosa (Wolf).

"Not all of the time, he seems to talk like Paleeto (Pal). Only the one he is talking to can hear him." she said. "It seems to be that way with a lot of different animals." she continued.

"Then why is it that I can hear most of what the birds are saying? asked Mozla (Jeff).

"Most birds will talk to whoever will lend an ear." she said laughing.

"Notnah (Not) says that sometimes birds talk too much, but then again they say a lot sometimes." said Rogna (Rodger).

"Well if we don't keep moving it will be late evening before we get to the camp." said Running Bear.

We started walking again, and as we did, everyone turned to say thanks to Notnah (Not). The language of the body let us all know that he accepted our thanks.

The rest of our trip went very well, but it was almost dark when we got in sight of Singing Sun's camp. One of the young braves saw us and the call went out. Soon some of the people came out to meet us and to walk with us into camp. They didn't seem at all shook that Notnah (Not) was walking along with us.

Healing Waters looked at me and giggled. "It is most common for our honored friend here, to walk into camp. He and his people are very special to all of us." she said pointing to Notnah (Not).

"They feel that their camp is very honored to have the presence of the ones you call Sasquatch. They are known to us, to hold very special powers and knowledge. But most of our peoples cannot speak to them as we can, but there is usually at least one that can receive the message being sent. If no one in Singing Sun's camp could hear Notnah (Not) or his people speak, then their message for them, would be given to us to take to Singing Sun." she continued.

"Oh, well, that all makes sense to me." I said as we all continued walking into the center of camp.

"Singing Sun! You look well." Running Bear said, greeting Singing Sun with a hug.

"Yes, our people are doing good now." said Singing Sun.

"Now? What is this Now, you speak of?" asked Two Wolves.

We all had an open ear to hear the stories that were about to unfold.

"Well come sit by the fire and have something to eat while we all tell you of the happenings of the last few pestrons (weeks)." he said.

We all sat down around the fire. It felt good, the evening was getting a little cool. While we were eating, a very cute little girl with large black eyes, rosy cheeks and long black braids came and sat down near us. Not long after she sat down and started to eat, a rather tall man came and sat down next to Singing Sun. We all sat and eat silently for a few keptrons (minutes).

"Oh yes," said Singing Sun, "All of you don't know who you're sitting next to. I have gathered all of the ones that have been effected by the happenings this last two pestrons (weeks) to eat with us and share their stories with you." he continued.

"This is Soaring Eagle," he said, pointing to the tall brave that had sat down next to him. He and his wife Dancing Doe are our shaman and this small one here," he said, pointing to the little girl, "is their daughter, she hasn't made a sound since the beam took her about two pestrons (weeks) ago. Her name is now Silent Dove, she was known as Laughing Dove. This is Two Rivers one of our best hunters and his wife Many Waters." he said, looking back at us.

We nodded hello and smiled greetings to all of them.

"You said something about a beam?" asked Running Bear.

"Yes, but I think we had better start at the beginning of all that has happened in the last few pestrons (weeks)." said Singing Sun.

"I guess I should be the one to start the telling of the tale." said Two Rivers, "I had decided to go night fishing. It was a quiet night and the moon was full. There were small patches of clouds but the sky was mostly clear. It was a good night for fishing. I had caught about five large fish and was waiting on the next one, when I saw flashes of light in the sky. I knew it wasn't lightning from a storm because the clouds weren't the stormy kind. I started to watch the skies to see where the flashes were coming from, that's when I saw the shiny flying thing. It was dodging and darting in and out of the trees, like it was chasing something. It started to get closer so I hid in some small trees near the water and watched. Soon a large buck came running through the trees and stopped nearby, another flash came and this one hit the buck in the head. He fell to the ground. A beam of light descended from the shiny thing in the sky and went all around him. Then all of a sudden there were three of these gray beings standing over him. Everything I saw after that showed dishonor to the buck and our Mother. One of them took this small beam of light and made a hole in the buck's side. Then another of the beings reached in and pulled out some of its organs and put them in a pan that one of the others was holding. I thought that was bad enough but then they went to the head of the buck. They used the beam again to cut through its skull. They took its brain and then left in the beam.

The horror of the whole situation was that the deer was aware of what was happening all the way through it. The deer was looking around and crying for help and I couldn't do anything to help. I felt pain in my heart for the deer, AWWW... The pain must have been horrendous for the buck. I would not want to be the being that will have to answer for this crime. At the end when the deer's brain was removed, Grandfather Owl came to get the deer, as they were entering the land of peace the deer was asking why? I didn't get to hear Grandfather Owl's answer. I still wonder why these beings are allowed to do these things." he said as he wiped a tear from his eye.

As he finished tell the story, you could still see the pain he was feeling from what he had witnessed. There were the fine streaks of moisture where a few tears had run down his cheeks.

"I guess I should tell our part next," said Soaring Eagle. "Dancing Doe and I were preparing the herbs for a sweat and Silent Dove was playing in the tall grass close to the camp with her friend, Whirling Wind, they were playing chase and laughing. I had just looked up from my work in time to see this beam of light come from the sky. Dancing Doe saw it at the same time and came running and screaming. We ran to where the light was but by the time we got there it was gone and so was Silent Dove. The rest of the tribe joined in the hunt for her the rest of the afternoon. But she wasn't found.

Not a sign of her. The beam had taken her."

Even in the telling of the story and his daughter sitting next to him, I could hear the fear and anguish in his voice. As I looked over at Dancing Doe, I could see tears building in her eyes.

"We all decided to hold a fasting prayer along with the sweat for the safe return of Silent Dove. We had all just gathered when another beam of light came from the sky almost like a flash. We all went toward where the light beam had been and found Silent Dove stumbling in the dark toward us. As I rushed to her I could see that she was bleeding from her mouth, nose and even her ears. When we got back to camp and took a closer look at her, she had bruises all over the lower part of her body. She looked dazed and didn't make a sound. We cleaned her up, fed her and held her till she fell asleep. Next amacron (morning) instead of her usual active self, she just lay in bed and stared off into nothingness, not moving and not making a sound. It was almost as if she was in a spell or trance. This went on for days, we had to feed her and take care of her just like as if she was a newborn. Then one evening there was a great storm. There was much lightening and loud thundering, after about the third set, Silent Dove got up from her bed and looked outside then back at us. We just knew that things were going to get better for her, but she still doesn't say words even now."

     "But she is learning ways to let us know what she wants," broke in Dancing Doe with a short smile on her lips.

     "Yes, it does seem as if her memory of knowing words was lost." Soaring Eagle continued. "I think this is where I will ask for your help. I have been told that you carry great knowledge and tools for these matters." he said as he looked straight at Strong Bow and me.

"Well, we will do what we can, but first we all need a good night sleep." I said.

"That sounds like a real good idea, it has been a long day," said Running Bear.

Chapter Eight
A Dream Me?

"Can we three stay up a little longer and watch the stars?" ask Elmosa (Wolf).

"Yes, I guess that will be alright, but not too late, ok?" I said.

"No, just a little while." said Elmosa (Wolf).

"I would like to know more about the stars too, if it is ok. Can I also stay up a little longer, Father," asked Morning Star.

He looked at Strong Bow and me then at the boys. We all nodded our ok.

"I think it might give them all a good chance to get better acquainted," said Strong Bow with a smile.

"Yes, it may at that. But not too late for you either daughter," said Running Bear looking back at Morning Star.

"*Come on Notnah (Not), your one of our party,*" said Morning Star.

  "Sure, come on, the more the better," said
Mozla (Jeff), motioning to Notnah (Not).
  Notnah (Not) turned and looked at
Running Bear and the others disappearing
into their tents for the night, then turning and
looked at the group that had claimed him as
one of theirs and you could almost see a smile
on his face. He closed the space between
them quickly.
  "Good, now since everyone is here, I
spotted that hill right over there earlier this
evening and I think it will be good for star
gazing," said Mozla (Jeff).
  Notnah (Not) ran ahead of the others
and laid down in the tall grass. He was on his
back flapping his arms and legs in the tall
grass, making almost a flat circle all around
him. When he finished he sat up and
motioned for the others to sit there with him.
They all smiled and sat down.
  "Morning Star? Would you mind if we
all ask you some questions?" asked Rogna
(Rodger).
  "Not, as long as I can ask all of you
some?" answered Morning Star.
  "Well, I want to know how old you
are." asked Mozla (Jeff).
  "I will be 16 when the Dogwood
blossoms this time," she answered.
  "And you are really the little sister of
Strong Bow, right?" asked Mozla (Jeff).

"Yes, I am," she said.

"Then that would make you Elmosa (Wolf)'s Aunt, wouldn't it?" continued Mozla (Jeff).

"Yes, I believe it does. Oh! that is good it means I have family from the stars," she said with a smile and almost a bounce in her words.

"Why does that make you so happy?" asked Mozla (Jeff) looking confused.

"Not everyone has family from the stars. It's like having a gift that no one else can have," she said.

"That makes good sense to me," said Rogna (Rodger) smiling.

"I feel that I already know you," said Elmosa (Wolf).

"Us too," said Rogna (Rodger) and Mozla (Jeff) together while glancing at each other. Morning Star looked confused now.

"Please explain how this could be. You only landed a few days ago?" asked Notnah (Not) in his own way.

"Well, it is sort of a long story, but I will try to make it as short as I can," said Elmosa (Wolf). "On the planet I was raised on, we have a building call a Creation Dome. In this place you could make anything happen that you wanted. So my father, Strong Bow, made a camp just like yours here and in this camp, you and all of your people lived. It was all sort of like a big dream place. But we learned a lot of your ways before we got here. Anyway my father programmed the compulink." Noting the confusion on Notnah (Not) and Morning Stars face, he tried to explain better. "A compulink is a machine, like a big box, you tell it what you want and it makes it happen. Anyway he told this box about you, Morning Star, your age, what you looked like the last time he seen you and the way you were being raised, and the box made a person that it thought would be like you the age you would have been then.," he explained.

"*Do you have one of these boxes with you now?*" asked Notnah (Not), "*Because I am hungry.*

Elmosa (Wolf) looked at Notnah (Not) for a few moments. "No, and it's not used for that sort of thing anyway." Elmosa (Wolf) said.

"I would have to say that the compulink did a real good job," said Rogna (Rodger) with a smile while looking at Morning Star.

"Yah, I think it did at that," said Mozla (Jeff) looking a Rogna (Rodger) with a grin.

"I mean it made the dream you, look enough like the real you that we knew who you were when we first seen you." said Elmosa (Wolf).

"Now I'm really confused," sighed Notnah (Not).

"Me too, sort of," Morning Star said scratching her head and wrinkling up her nose. "A dream me and a real me? I am me and that is all."

"Don't you say a word, I'm warning you now," said Rogna (Rodger) looking back at Mozla (Jeff).

Mozla (Jeff) looked at Rogna (Rodger) like as if he was going to tell Morning Star about the crush Rogna (Rodger) had on her. He loved teasing Rogna (Rodger) anytime he thought he could get a rise from him.

"Well like I said, it is hard to explain. I guess it is just one of those things you would have to see." said Elmosa (Wolf) looking at Morning Star then at Mozla (Jeff) who was starting to laugh.

Rogna (Rodger) turned and gave Mozla (Jeff) "that's enough" look and Mozla (Jeff) almost fell over with laughter. They had both forgotten that Notnah (Not) was telepathic and had gotten the gist of what was going on.

"Oooo... That makes me feel all warm," sighed Notnah (Not) while crossing his arms and rocking himself.

"What is going on you guys, this isn't fair, you have to tell," demanded Morning Star.

"Well, it's a little awkward to say right out," stammered Elmosa (Wolf). "I mean another time would be better,"

"*I'll tell, I want to tell, I know, I know,*" Notnah (Not) said almost jumping in place.

"This is your last chance guys, someone had better tell me." she demanded as she stood up.

Then she looked at Notnah (Not) and he was just ready to say something and both Rogna (Rodger) and Mozla (Jeff) looked at him.

"*No! It's not your place to tell.*" both Rogna (Rodger) and Mozla (Jeff) said telepathically.

"*I will be the one to let her know.*" continued Rogna (Rodger).

Notnah (Not) looked at Morning Star and hung his head, "*I cannot tell you, it is not my place. I am feeling bad because I can't help you.*" he said.

"It's okay, I will find out and understand about these machines someday." said Morning Star as she glanced back at the boys, turned and stalked off towards camp.

All of the guys just sat there for a few moments sort of stunned that she had walked off.

"Rogna (Rodger), you had better go explain things or she will be angry with all of

us and we are going to be here for a while
yet." said Elmosa (Wolf).

"I agree." said Mozla (Jeff).

"*Me too,*" chimed in Notnah (Not).

Rogna (Rodger) stood and looked at
the rest of his friends then towards Morning
Star, his heart was starting to beat wildly.

"Go, we will wait here and watch the
stars till you get back," said Mozla (Jeff).

Rogna (Rodger) took off running to
catch Morning Star before she got to camp,
his heart beating so fast he felt as if it would
out run him.

"Wait Morning Star," he said as he
caught up with her." I want to explain what
was going on back there." he said pointing at
the top of the hill. "But I'm not sure where to
start."

"Just start at the beginning," she said.

"Let's sit over here on this log and I
will try to tell where I first met you. Okay?"
he said.

"Okay," said Morning Star a little
calmer now.

"Well, back on Cyterrious where I
have lived most of my life, we have machines
that can do almost anything we ask. Well,
they have one of those machines in a place
that we call the Creation Domes. Strong Bow
had this machine create a camp just like the
one he live and have grown up in here on

Earth. He told the machine about the ways of the land and the animals. He told it about all the people in his tribe, the way all of you lived, and your rules of life. He described each member of the tribe and the machine created a person that looked and acted just the way he remembered them. Then he told the machine all about you, you were only three when he left Earth, but the machine made your look alike the age you would be in real time. So in the Creation Dome we had a chance to meet you and each tribal member, while pretty much growing up together, and the last time I was in the creation domes was just before we came here. In the dome you were just as you are now, here. The creations were close enough that we all knew who everyone was when we first landed, it was almost like being home. In the Dome you and I had a lot of fun, I thought you were very pretty when I first saw you standing under a tree near the stream. We became real good friends." he said with a slight smile. "Then when we landed and I saw that you were real, I thought that I was dreaming. Here I was really going to get to meet you and really get to know you! I fell in love with your people and your way of living in the Domes! But to really be here now! I am so happy. I want to live here with you and your people." he said reaching for her hand.

"What are you saying?" she asked.

"I am saying I want to live here on Earth with you. I want to be part of your people." he said.

"My people have a strict code to live by. You have to past the tests of the elders before they will give you permission to stay with us and be one with our people." she explained.

"When I pass all of their test then can I ask you to be one with me." he said shyly.

"Are you asking me to marry you?" she asked.

"Yes please, it would make me feel complete. I feel I already know you." he said looking into her eyes.

"First the tests then we will see if the courting will be, but as it stand right now I feel you have a good chance." she said with a giggle.

"Shall we go back and tell the others? They are waiting on top of the hill for us." he said.

As they walked back up the hill together, Rogna (Rodger) reached over and put his arm around her. She looked over at him with a slight smile.

As they came closer to where the others were, she took Rogna (Rodger)'s arm from around her and stopped for a moment.

She looked into his eyes. "We cannot say anything about us getting married yet, because you have to past the tests of the counsel. Do you understand why? And I want to know more about you, after all you have had sectos (years) with my dream self." she said.

"Not really." he said.

"Well, when two of our young people fall in love, first the parents are told then they go to the counsel and ask for permission, when it is given then it becomes official and then the rest of the tribe is told." she said.

"Okay, I won't mention the marriage but I can tell them that there is a good chance that I may be staying here, Okay?" he ask. "I mean after all they are my best friends."

"Okay, but they must keep it a secret till we tell our parents and the Council." she said.

"Good, they can do that. We have many secrets." he said.

"Hey guys, we're back." said Rogna (Rodger) as they walked toward their friends holding hands.

"Oh, I see you two came to an understanding." said Mozla (Jeff) with a grin.

"Well, yes, I guess one could say that." said Rogna (Rodger) with a smile while he and Morning Star exchanged looks.

"We must head back to camp, it is getting really late and we all have to get up early tomorrow, before the sun. There is to be a big hunt for game. Each sectos (year) some of our best hunters join with the hunters of Singing Sun's to gather meat for both camps. You will be meeting the other hunters in Singing Sun's camp early." said Morning Star.

"But we want to know what is happening with you two." said Elmosa (Wolf).

"*Oh I can tell you that.*" said Notnah (Not).

"I have an idea, but I want to hear it in their own words." said Elmosa (Wolf).

"I will tell you all, in the amacron (morning)." said Rogna (Rodger) as he and Morning Star turned and strolled down the hill holding hands.

Running Bear was on his way up the hill and met all of the kids on their way down.

"Father, I need to talk to you." said Morning Star.

"Well I can see something is going on." he said with a slight smile.

"How is that?" she asked.

"Oh, by the way you look and act," he said, "so tell me what all of you have been up to."

"We were all looking at the skies and talking, then Rogna (Rodger) and I got to talking and ahhh." she started stumbling over words.

"Well sir, I would like to become part of the tribe and wed Morning Star." spoke up Rogna (Rodger).

"Strong Bow has told me of the program he made in this place called the Creation Domes on your world and of the people in it. I sort of thought this would happen. I will be proud to have you as a son, but you first have to pass the test of the Inner Counsel and become a part of the tribe." he said.

Now the rest of the group had just walked up at the tail end of the conversation.

"Test for what Grandfather?" asked Elmosa (Wolf).

"Rogna (Rodger) wants to become part of our family, but he will first have to be tested by the Council of Elders." Running Bear explained.

"Oh I think he will be able to past all of the test. We have all practiced in the Domes on Cyterrious." Elmosa (Wolf) said with a smile.

"We'll see, but right now it is time for all of you to be asleep." said Running Bear as they all walked into camp together.
"Tomorrow is the great hunt of the sectos

(year). And all that are going on the hunt will be meeting in the center of camp at first light." he added.

"Can I go hunting with the others tomorrow?" asked Notnah (Not).

"I didn't know that your people hunted." said Elmosa (Wolf).

"Well, we really don't hunt in the same way as you mean but with us it is more of a game. We go into the forest and keep track of all the animals we can find without them seeing us, and the one with the most wins. But I have learned to track real good. So can I go?" asked Notnah (Not) again.

"We will have to ask the Elders and see what they say. I cannot give an answer tonight. So good night and I will see all of you at first light." said Running Bear waving good night as the boys went into their shelter for the night. "Come Morning Star, first light will come fast and we must rest."

Chapter Nine
The Great Hunt

First light rushed in with drumming, dancing and lots of songs. The young hunters from Running Bear's camp and ours had gotten there just as the sun's first rays were just peeking above the valley floor to the east.

The central fire was started at the first official light. The drumming started at first sight of Running Bear's hunting party. One could say that with the rising of the sun, the spirit of everyone in the camp intensified that amacron (morning).

This was a very important day for all of the people from both camps. The hunt this day would determine the food supply in the hardest part of the winter to come. All of the people had been preparing for this for pestrons (weeks). All of the tools were sharp and ready. The racks were built and the bowls and herbs were waiting.

We had all been singing the praises of and to our Mother and Father Creator Parents and asking for a great hunt. And the sun was just coming up over the ridge and we could all see really well into the forest now.

All of those going on the hunt were to be sent out in groups, each hunting in different places.

"Now do we go? I mean can I go?" asked Notnah (Not) looking at Running Bear.

"Yes, you may go, I asked for you and they said you can go with Strong Bow, the boys and me." said Running Bear.

Notnah (Not) was almost jumping with joy, he was so pleased.

All of the hunters were given a ration of food for the day and Morning Star handed Notnah (Not) a leather pouch of herbs, fresh vegetables and fruit after we all shared our first meal of the(sestron) day.

"Well, are we all ready? asked Singing Sun and Running Bears at the same time, while looking at all of the hunters standing in a circle around them.

"YES!" came an energetic answer from all the hunters at once.

"The Elders have arranged all of you in groups and have given you the direction for your hunting, good hunting be with all of us." said Singing Sun as he waved his hand to all and left with his group.

"That was a wise move on the part of the council, I mean putting the hunter into groups. Especially with the trouble we've all been having with the others that have the hot beams and all." I said.

"Yes, very wise." said Healing Waters, "And that is why they are our the Council of Elders."

"While we waited on one of the hunting parties to bring in their first catch, we finished preparing a few more herbs for curing the meat and furs.

Healing Waters explained to the younger women, that this hunt was very important to both camps. "These kinds of hunts bring unity to our camps and helped in providing food and warmth for the winters."

Our wait was ended shortly after noon, when three of the brave from the north party came into camp with the first deer to be taken care of. They left the deer in the center of camp and took off again to join the rest of their party.

By early afternoon everyone had brought back something. Even Notnah (Not) was carrying something over one shoulder when he came into camp. When he got closer we could all see that he had been fishing. He was carrying a long vine full of very large fish.

"I went hunting too. See!" he said proudly holding up all the fish he had caught.

Healing Waters told the rest of the people what Notnah (Not) said, because there were some who couldn't hear him.

"I can see you did and I have to say, you did a very good job of it too." I said.

"I couldn't bring myself to hunt the other animals to be killed." he said. "I tried, I stayed with the group through the first kill but I couldn't stand the look in the eyes of the one dying. So I went fishing. My people fish all the time, so I am good at it. So I did that while everyone else hunted close by." he continued.

"That fine, you did a good job today." said Healing Waters who had been standing next to me.

"Are you going out with the hunters again tomorrow?" I asked.

"I really don't want too. Can I stay here around the camp and pick berries?" he said.

"I don't see any reason why you can't, in fact you could stay near the children tomorrow." Dancing Doe spoke up with a smile.

Just then Running Bear's party brought in two large bucks.

"I think this will be enough for today." said Running Bear with a big smile.

"All of you did a good job today! We are all very proud of all of us! Now for the feast and stories of today's hunt!" announced Singing Sun.

"I was wondering when you were coming in. It was starting to get dark." I said while giving Strong Bow and Elmosa (Wolf) a hug.

"I know we are late getting in, but father felt that he needed this last big buck to finish the day. You know how he is about hunting." said Strong Bow.

"Let's eat, I'm starving!" Elmosa (Wolf) announced.

"We can talk later, let's go listen to the stories of the day." Strong Bow said then gave me a kiss.

After everyone had eaten and the last story had been told everyone went to sleep, dreaming of good hunting. Many of the younger hunter slept near the fire.

Daylight came fast and it wasn't long after that before everyone that was hunting, was gone and the children were picking berries and playing. We could hear their laughter and Notnah (Not)'s sounds of joy.

It looked like it was going to turn out to be a good day for hunting. By noon the count of deer was already at 12 and the rabbits were counted at 15 plus 6 squirrels. It looked like the winter food was almost taken care of.

Chapter Ten
Notnah (Not) Saves the Children

Then there was a blood-curdling scream. And it sounded as if it came from the direction of the river. Then it hit me like a load of rock, right in the pit of my stomach. That's the area where the children were playing.

I looked around camp. All of the women were standing very still. No one wanted to move till we knew for sure where the sound was coming from.

There it was again and I could hear Notnah (Not)'s message trailing the scream.

"Bear, Big Bear! Come Quick! Help!" screamed Notnah (Not) telepathically.

Healing Water grabbed a largest pole that she could manage. While Dancing Doe and some of the others grabbed rocks that were fist size.

I went in and grabbed my Crystal Array Kayits from my pack. *'God, I haven't shot this since Bent Twig died by the paw of a bear. I hope I can still shoot straight'.* I thought while making sure it was charging on my way to Notnah (Not).

I ran down the path to the river as fast as I could. As I rounded the bend in the path near the clearing, I saw Healing Waters wielding the pole toward the bear. She got his attention okay by hitting him in the back of the head. Now he was angry and lunged at Healing Waters. Then Dancing Doe stepped in and the rest of the women, all throwing rocks at the same time. I climbed up into a nearby tree where I could get a good shot off without taking a chance on shooting anyone else. This was a big bear and so I made sure the CAK was set on a setting a little over half of its full force.

I took careful aim and fired. It was a hit, but it wasn't good enough to kill the bear. Now he was really upset. I had hit him in the neck. I fired again and this time I got him in the side. He turned toward me and now I knew I had to set the CAK near the higher settings. My hand was shaking now as I pushed the slide all the way to its highest force just below disintegration. Then I propped my arm on the limb, aimed for the head and fired. It was a good hit and none too soon. He fell to the ground with a thundering thud and only two feet in front of me.

I took a deep breath of relief as I set the CAK in the locked position. As I climbed down out of the tree, I saw Notnah (Not) out of the corner of my eye coming toward me. He looked relieved too.

"I am glad you had that thing in your hand, it made the bear die. He tried to kill all of us. I tried to talk to him, but he was already angry when he came to the river. I think he ate something that poisoned his mind." said Notnah (Not).

"Well, if you hadn't yelled when you did there is a good chance that he may have killed one of you." I said, patting Notnah (Not) on the back.

"Yes, thank you Notnah (Not)." said Healing Waters and Dancing Doe at almost the same time.

The rest of the women were busy working on the bear.

"You know Healing Waters, it looks like we have a story to tell tonight." I said.

"Maybe so, but we must keep it less dramatic than the stories the men have." she said.

I must have given her a questioning look.

"Think about it, if we make our adventure sound good, then it will more than likely make some of their stories sound, well not so great. And that would most likely cause trouble. And put the women in competition

with the men and we don't want that." she
said.

"Oh, when you put it that way, a short
quick story would do just fine." I said, "Maybe
we can tell our adventure last." I added..

We all hurried and carved up the bear
so we could get it back to camp before any of
the men came back in.

Some of the women had stayed in
camp, this way if any of the hunters came in
with their kills they could take care of them.

When Notnah (Not) said it was a big
bear, he wasn't kidding. It towered over him.
He was only about half the bear's height.

Notnah (Not) helped me, Healing
Water, and Dancing Doe carry the bear into
camp. After we skinned the bear it took four
of the women to carry fur to one of the larger
stretching racks some of the younger women
made.

Not long after we got everything under
control again the hunters started coming into
camp with the last of the kills.

No one said anything about the bear till
story telling time later that night after
everyone had eaten, then Notnah (Not)
couldn't hold back any more.

*"We had a visit by a big bear today and
Elaytay (Tay) killed it with that buzzing thing she
holds in her hand."* he said with Strong Bow

telling the rest of the group that couldn't hear what was being sent.

"So where is the fur?" asked Singing Sun.

"It's being cured and stretched." said Dancing Doe.

And then of course everyone had to go see it.

"That is a very huge bear mom." said Elmosa (Wolf).

"Well this is after it's been stretched." I said.

"You can stretch a fur all you want but it will only get so big and I would have to say, this was a great kill for our people and the timing was good." said Singing Sun. "And the fur will go to Running Bear." he continued.

"This has been a good hunt and the women were good hunters too this season." said Two Wolves with a smile. "And a very large thank you to Notnah (Not) for alerting the women to the danger of the bear." he continued.

"Yes, we all agree. Thank you Notnah (Not)!" said Singing Sun raising his hand for the unity of the whole group.

Everyone came and said thanks to Notnah (Not) in groups. And this took the attention off the women.

"I think everyone from our camp would do good to get some rest now.

Amacron (morning) will come soon. We all must be ready to make the trip back to our camp and we will all have something to carry." said Running Bear.

Running Bear was right. Amacron (morning) did come early and I still felt tired but we had to pack up everything we had brought and then we had to pack up our camp's share of the meat and furs from the great hunt. We were lucky that most of the meat and furs had lost a lot of their water weight through the drying process of the last two days. So they were a little lighter now than they would have been if they were fresh. Some of our hunters stayed behind and waited for the meat and furs to dry a little more before carrying them to our camp. But even at that, all of us were carrying back pretty much twice the weight we brought in with us.

Soon we were on our way back to our home camp. One of the young men in the group ran ahead to tell the women when we got within a short distant from the camp. When the call went out to them, they came out to meet us and help carry back the meats and furs.

Almost all of the women of Running Bear's camp stayed in camp while we went to Singing Sun's for the hunt. They were making ready everything that was need for the finishing touches of curing the meats and furs. This way there wasn't any time lost in the curing of the meat and furs.

"It seemed that we had quite a good hunt this sectos (year)." One of the young women said that was helping to carry everything back to camp.

It was almost dark before everything calmed down and was back to normal. We had a good dinner and story time.

Most of us went to sleep early that night because of all the energy we had been putting out all the other days during the hunt. Even Notnah (Not) went to sleep early. Next amacron (morning) I could tell everything was back to normal. Everyone was up early and real hungry. This looked to be a very promising day.

After we ate, I went out into the surrounding area to take some soil samples. After all, the small plants we had brought with us were ready to be thinned out and transplanted into a larger area so they could spread out.

Chapter Eleven
Exploring a Cavern

While I was out taking samples, I found a cave. Keeping this in mind I took the soil samples back to camp and made a fast check of them. It turned out that the area I had gotten the samples from was a good place to transplant a lot of the plants we had brought with us.

Most of the women and about half of the men of our camp spent the rest of the day transplanting the small seedlings.

Meanwhile back in camp, Elmosa (Wolf) and Mozla (Jeff) had gone with Rogna (Rodger) and Chief Running Bear, to see the Council of Elders about letting Rogna (Rodger) become part of the tribe.

That evening after dinner I told Strong Bow about the cave I had found. I knew the rules. No one is to explore a cave or areas like that unless it was done with someone else. So early the next amacron (morning), I asked if anyone wanted to go exploring with me. But Notnah (Not) was the only one that wasn't really doing anything real important.

I gathered up the equipment I knew we would need for cave exploring, then Notnah (Not) and I set out to explore the cave.

Exploring caves to me was like opening a gift from someone special. You never really knew what you were going to find inside it.

The cave wasn't far from camp, so Strong Bow felt we would be safe enough.

When we got in sight of the cave entrance, I noticed that it was a little higher up the side of the cliff than what I had remembered.

I sat my backpacks down at the foot of the cliff

"Why are we stopping?" asked Notnah (Not).

"We will need clamp-ons for this slope." I said. Notnah (Not) looked puzzled. "Like these... they are like claws, so we don't slide back down the slope and lose ground." I tried explaining and holding up a pair of clamp-ons.

"I don't need them. I have 'clamp-ons' already. See!" he said holding up one foot and wiggling his toes.

"Yes, you do and better ones than me." I said laughing. "We'd better grab the packs and get started if we want to see much of the cave." I said as I finished securing the last strap.

We climbed steadily up the large mound of rock that looked as if it had fallen from the cliffs above the cave.

As we reached the opening of the cave, we were hit with a wave of dank musty air.

"Urg!...*It smells like its' been sealed off from the outside for a long time."* said Notnah (Not)

"I think you may be right, those rocks look like they have fallen not too long ago." I said pointing at the rocks we had just climbed up. *"I'll go in first."*

I took off my pack and went through the opening then pulled my pack through the opening after me.

"I hope you can make it through the cave opening because there is plenty of room inside." I said.

I could see by the silhouette that Notnah (Not) was pushing his pack through first. Then it got really dark in the cave and I had to turn on my headlamp in order to see.

Notnah (Not) first tried to come through the opening just by stooping over, but that didn't work. Then he tried coming through sideways and that didn't work.

"Notnah (Not)! You may have to crawl through the opening on your hands and knees." I said. I could see that he was starting to get upset.

"Good you made it through. We will have to remember the crawling technique on the way out of this cave." I said with a smile.

"I think I am getting bigger." he said.

"Well of course you are, and you will get even bigger before long. Let's go see the rest of this cave." I said patting him on the back.

I helped Notnah (Not) put a travel lamp on his head and we stood for a few microns (seconds) and looked around.

The colors inside was almost like looking at a crystal rainbow. As we shined our lamp lights on the walls they glistened like the diamond of fresh fallen rain on beautifully colored flower peddles.

I shined my light down into the middle room of the cavern below us and there I found a small waterfall trickling from just above a golden ridge on one wall in the higher end of the room.

We made our way carefully toward the waterfall while laying out a track line behind, us so we could follow it back on our way out.

As we got closer to the small waterfall I could see that it was running into a small pool at the base of the wall. But the pool wasn't getting any deeper and it wasn't over running the edges of the pool like a stream.

"There must be a lower room to this cave." I said. *"Look, the water has to be going somewhere."* I continued, while pointing at the pool.

Then upon closer examination of the waterfall, I found a clear blue crystal about half the size of my hand poking out from behind the water. I wanted to get a better look so I thought I would just remove a little of the dirt around it. But when I started to remove the dirt the water started running faster, and faster. Now it was running so fast that it had filled up the pool and was now filling the lowest parts of the cavern room we were in. Soon the water was coming over the tops of my boots and Notnah (Not) wanted to leave.

Just as he started to make his way back to the upper room to the opening of the cave, the wall gave way and the next thing I knew, I was being knocked down by a rushing wall of water. I soon found myself standing in knee deep water.

Then I turned to look where the wall once stood and there right in front of me was the most breathtaking scene I could have ever imagined.

It was like a secret world. The walls were clearly not naturally made. They were straight and tall, with a hint of beige coloring, sprinkled with silver dust that sparkled like stars. There were paintings on the walls of flowers that I had never seen before. Also of birds with colors that would shame a rainbow. The whole area was lit up and we didn't need our headlamps, so we turned them off.

Notnah (Not) had just caught up with me as I stepped up into the room to have a closer look.

"I don't know if anyone will believe us... about seeing all of this! I mean it's going to be hard to explain." I said.

"What is this place?" ask Notnah (Not). *"I heard a lot of stories but none of them included a place like this one."* he continued.

I looked back over my shoulder at him. *"I have no idea, but I plan to find out. You may want to stay close by me."* I said.

Notnah (Not) spent no time getting next to me. As he took that last step to close the gap, I caught sight of a picture of the most brilliantly colored bird with its' wings spread and a ruby for its' eye. I started toward it so I could see it better. As I reached out my hand to touch its' eye Notnah (Not) grabbed my arm and growled.

"*What? Why did you stop me and why did you growl?*" I asked.

"*I didn't remember any stories about a room like this, but I do remember stories about a red eyed bird that kills those who come in contact with it.*" he said.

I hadn't noticed it before, but when Notnah (Not) grabbed my arm and swung it around it must have triggered something. Because now in the middle of the room there was a hologram of what some may call an elder or a leader of some sort.

The rather tall gentle looking humanoid had long dark wavy hair to his shoulders and large dark emerald green eyes. He was wearing white robes trimmed in gold and had on what looked to be leather sandals. He was speaking in a rather strange language at first. Then after listening closer I found it to be one of the dialects on Debon 4 in the Stanic system.

He introduced himself as Arnic (Arnold) and was saying something about his group landing on Earth about three hundred sectos (years) ago and making their homes under ground because of the large animals that roamed the surface. The red eyed bird I was going to touch was a picture of the only animal they had brought with them. On

Debon 4 these birds were kept as guard birds
for important places and would kill intruders.
I was welcomed to their city and told how to
proceed.

Chapter Twelve
Finding the Lost City

It seemed that the wave of my arm activated the censors and that was what was needed to gain entrance to the city. The picture of the bird with the bright red eye was the guardian for this city.

The humanoid vanished and my attention was drawn back to Notnah (Not) tugging at my sleeve.

"What did the man say?" he asked.

"You didn't understand him?" I said surprised. *"I thought that you were able to read thoughts no matter what language was used."*

"The picture had no thoughts, just words for you to understand." he explained.

"Oh yes, of course. I wasn't thinking, it was just a hologram and there is no thought process with pictures. Well, he said "welcome to their city" and told me how to get into the heart of the city." I explained.

Notnah (Not) gave me a most curious look. *"Can I go to the city with you?"* he asked.

"Yes of course. but I think you will have to stay real close to me. But first I think we need to write a note to the others and let them know what is happening, along with the warning not to touch the red eye of the bird." I said.

I took a pen and paper from my pack and wrote a note to Strong Bow and the others explaining everything so far. Then I sent Notnah (Not) to the opening of the cave with it to be put in a place where someone would find it, if they came looking for us.

He had placed it part way under one of the clamp-ons I had brought for him.

When he got back to me, he was wet from his knees down. It seems that the middle room was made to hold the water overflows that came into the cave. I looked over at the small pool that the water was collecting in earlier and it was back to normal. But the water was still draining to another place below the floor somewhere.

Notnah (Not) had notices something else on his way back to me, in the upper room where I was waiting for him. As he came closer to me he started to point toward the red eyed bird.

I turned and noticed a wall panel protruding from under the bird's left wing with dials and switches on it.

"This must have been what Arnic (Arnold) was talking about." I said looking at Notnah (Not). "Now how did that go again? Was it turn the left one to the left five turns and the middle switch up to the right or was it the right dial three turns to the right and the lower switch up and to the left?" I said thinking out loud.

"Don't you remember?" asked Notnah (Not) looking worried.

"Not to worry Notnah (Not), I turned on the vox recorder when Arnic (Arnold) first started to talk. See." I said holding up the vox box as I chuckled.

"That's not funny. We are in a strange place with many strange things and there is a death warning on the red bird. Don't be funny!" said Notnah (Not).

"Okay, I promise I'll smile from now on before I play or tease with you while we are in dangerous places." I said.

I turned on the vox to the beginning so I could get the directions straight. Then I proceeded to turn the right dial to the left four turns and the lower right switch down and then to the right. Then I turned the left dial to the right two turns then back to the left three more after flipping the middle switch to the up and back to the center position. The lower left switch was to be flipped down and then back to the center position also.

Just as I had return the last switch to the center position the wall behind us started to slide back to show a long passage lit of both sides with glowing stones..

"Auhhh, *I don't like all these moving things.*" said Notnah (Not) making a strange face.

"*It will be ok, I think it's almost to a stopping point. See it's stopped moving. Okay?*" I said trying to ease Notnah (Not)'s mind. "Yeah, but I still don't like this place very much.

"*There's no sunlight down here.*" said Notnah (Not).

"*Stay close to me this is the way that Arnic (Arnold) said we were to go.*" I said.

As we walked down the dimly lit passage, we could feel the air getting cooler and the ground sloping at a slight downward angle. As we went deeper into the ground I could see and even feel Notnah (Not)'s agitation growing with every step.

Just then the passage opened into a large room with more pictures on the walls. There were pictures of very large animals I had never seen except in the history museum's videe files. Some of the pictures were of these animals eating each other while others were eating plants. Then there was a picture of everything being dark and in the next picture all of the plants looked almost dead and most all of the large animals were gone. Then the next few pictures were of Arnic (Arnold)'s people greeting other people who were landing here. Then pictures of all of them meeting a strange looking hairy creature standing up right like the others, and offering them what looked like large leaves and fruit.

"Look! Those are my people on the hills in the background. Our stories say we landed here and decided to study all of these beings for a while. Just to see what they were like before meeting them, and it was a good thing too... You see the hairy creature in this picture with the long tail curled around the log behind him? Well he and his people aren't around anymore. All these beings mated with them and they are what you find all over this planet now." explained Notnah (Not).

"Are you saying that the hairy creature in this picture and these other people we are looking at are the great, great, great, grandparents of this planet?" I asked while looking straight at Notnah (Not).

"Yes, If I've been told the stories right." he said nodding.

"That's odd, according to all the stories about the beginning that I have heard from the different planets I have visited, were of a Great Power creating a male and female and that is how we all got here." I said.

"Maybe that did happen at one time somewhere on another planet. I don't know about

those things. I just know the stories I was told."
said Notnah (Not)

I looked around at the rest of the room. On the floor about ten paces in front of me and to the right was a stone that was glowing a bright purple color.

"Look Notnah (Not), there's the stone Arnic (Arnold) talked about. Stay real close to me, because when I step on that stone there is supposed to be a large bright light and then we will be in a different part of the city." I said as Notnah (Not) reached out and grabbed my hand.

As I placed my foot on the stone, Notnah (Not) put both arms around me almost getting me in a bear hug, then the light rays hit both of us and we were in a different place.

"How are we going to get home, back up there where the sun is?" ask Notnah (Not) looking worried.

"I was given instructions, don't worry, we'll get back." I said trying to reassure him.

"You can let go of me now, so we can look around." I said, sort of peeling his hands free.

The whole area was bright. It was almost like as if they had captured part of the sun.

"They have the sun here too, but there is dirt over our heads. I don't understand." said Notnah (Not).

"I'm not sure what the power source is but there must be one for them to have this much energy this deep underground. I'm sure we will learn more in a little while." I said.

Notnah (Not) and I looked around without moving for a while. Arnic (Arnold)'s instructions were hard to understand. He had said something about when we got ready to leave we had to push a green button and turning a large red wheel, then we had 15 seconds to be standing on a blue cylinder with another over us.

As I looked around the area, all I saw was a court yard with nice building and a few walkways leading off into other parts on the city. Each of the buildings had very detailed carvings on them.

"Let's go and explore since we're here." I said looking over my shoulder at Notnah (Not).

"I just want to go back to where my sun shines." Notnah (Not) said almost looking frightened.

"We will be okay. Besides we need to find a few things in order to get home." I said motioning for him to follow me. *"Let's look in some of the buildings and see what there is."* I continued as Notnah (Not) caught up with me.

Within a short span of time we had looked inside of three of the buildings. In one of the buildings there was a machine with dishes around them and a few crumbs of food on some tables in the center of the main room. In another there were large amounts of folded cloth and a few garments on some shelves in one corner. While in the third, there were books and disks.

"This is the last large building that is close to us. Maybe the green button, red wheel and blue cylinders are in this one." I said.

Just as we got to the last building we heard a crashing sound from what looked to be a living area. It was a small building with windows.

"Let's go see what that was." I said turning toward the small building.

"I don't want to know, I just want to go home! Up there!" Notnah (Not) said pointing up.

Just then another crash came from the same area.

"Then you stay here, while I go see what it was." I said walking closer to the house.

"Wait for me!" Notnah (Not) said with a slight outer squeal, while running to catch up with me. *"I'm not staying anywhere down here by myself."*

As I entered the small building, I caught sight of a fleeting form out of the corner of my eye.

"Did you see it? Did you see what it was?" I asked looking over at Notnah (Not).

"Wha....? I didn't see anything, except what might have been a living area." he said marching in place.

"There it is again... I didn't see it clearly this time either, but it is making plenty of noise." I said.

"Your just seeing things and I want to go home." said Notnah (Not).

Just then a stack of small boxes that were on the table near Notnah (Not) fell over, brushing his arm on their way to the floor.

He yelped and jumped back a few paces.

"Oh, I'm just seeing things huh?" I said teasingly. "Well...I'm going to find out what or who is still living here and how they got here. If we're lucky and it's a who... they may know where the green button is. Or maybe there is another way to the surface." I continued then pausing to take a look back at Notnah (Not).

He was sitting on the table with his eyes closed and breathing very slowly.

"What are you doing?" I asked.

"I'm trying to get in sync with the who's' thought patterns....But I need a little bit of time and quiet." explained Notnah (Not).

So I sat down beside him very quietly and waited for what seemed to be a long time. Then all of a sudden it seemed that the sounds were getting closer and in more than one direction.

I opened my eyes and there standing in front of me and Notnah (Not) where several of these hairy creatures just slightly shorter than me. They all had tails and looked sort of like the monakee creatures on Pensna (a planet in the 3rd star system)

They were all looking at Notnah (Not).

He opened his eyes about then and jumped with a start.

"I can understand them pretty well now and they seem to understand what I am saying. Their language is very strange to me and it may take a while to get the answers to our questions." he said.

"First I want to know who they are and what, how and if....okay?" I said.

He seemed intrigued to have found others here he could talk telepathically to.

"Sure, go ahead and learn what you can and then let me know. While you're doing that I'm going to look around a little more. There seems to be a few rooms over there." I said pointing to the wall behind him.

Notnah (Not) looked at me over his shoulder and nodded.

Chapter Thirteen
Meeting Starneah (Star)

As I started for the other side of the room, I felt a tug on one sleeve. I looked down to see a smaller one of the creatures that we had just met.

"My name is Starneah (Star)." she said.

I was going to say something to Notnah (Not), but then I realized that I was able to understand this one. We made friends fast and Starneah (Star) was full of stories that her grandfather had told her.

"Some of our people were on the first ship to land here. We had to quickly make our way under the top layers because of all the large animals that were here." she said, with a slight smile.

"There are passages like this one and cities like this one all over this planet and some of them are connected to each other. They were all to be connected but something happened, and everything changed. The large animals started to

*die and when any of us went to the top to see
why, well they died too. Some of the elders said
they thought it was something in the air. But for
us not to worry about that because they had
machines to clean the air before we breathed it.
And that they were connected to the earth and
would never quit, and so far they haven't. We
grow all our own food, we have plenty of water
and good air, and even sunlight with the use of
what one elder call fiberflextion."* she
continued as she opened the door in front of
us.

*"Come on in and I'll show you our beach
area."* she said motioning for me to hurry.

As I walked into the next room I was
really amazed. There was a huge cavern
and in the center was a large area of
sunlight. As we grew closer to the sunny
spot, I could see that there were birds, trees,
flowers and fresh water flowing from a
spring into a small lake type area. I looked
back at Starneah (Star), who was about two
paces behind me, smiling.

*"Didn't the bad air come into your area
through this place?"* I asked.

*"No, during that time the elders seen fit
to place a large dome like protection field over
this area. That is why the walls of the earth
leading to the upper areas is so smooth."* she
explained with a smile. *"Come on and I will*

 she said taking me by the hand and almost dragging me.

We went back the way we came then through another door just before we left the area we were in. As I stood just inside the room it took a few moments for my eyes to adjust to the darkness. Then there it was just as plain as the nose on my face. In the ceiling were all the stars you could see if you were on top at night. Somehow their elders had rounded the ceiling of this room and put in the stars, and they even twinkled like the real ones.

"We must get back to the others, they have news for us." she said tugging at one arm.

Turning to walk out of the room I stumbled and almost fell over one of the sitting boulders they used for chairs.

When we came back into the room where all the others and Notnah (Not) was, they all turned to look at us.

Notnah (Not) got up to meet me. *"It seems that their people and my own people were travelers in the same way and that they all knew about each other and visited quite often. That is the reason I can understand them and we can talk."* he said.

"Well, I can understand Starneah (Star)." I said nodding toward her.

"I know you can there were those who only chose to speak in their own tongue and then there were others that wanted to learn other languages too. And Starneah (Star) happens to be from a family that made a point to learn additional languages like that of the ship masters they came with and other of them made it a point just to keep their own language alive. You see after the first ship landed here and they made their way underground to safety they sent out messages to the other ships and they brought others who wanted to settle a new land. They brought equipment and machines and all kinds of supplies so they could set all this up to last forever. Then there were those who came just to steal what they wanted and leave everything else to die. That is the reason for the special panels and switches. If the area is entered in the wrong way then all of the paths will lead into empty rooms and dead ends." Notnah (Not) explained.

"Your people are worried about you and you must return to them quickly." said one of the elders patting Notnah (Not) on the back.

"But it took us decons (hours) to get here." I said.

It was then that I understood what Notnah (Not) meant about some knowing both languages and that some were able to speak to both of us at the same time.

"Come, I will show you a way to the top that is quick and you can come visit again when

you want to." Starneah (Star) said grabbing me and Notnah (Not) by the hands and leading us up a side trail.

We walked steadily uphill the whole distance, going through different doors in different areas every few turns. I noticed that Starneah (Star) was pressing stones that were in bedded around the doors. Then we finally got to the top and she pushed up on the last door and we all climbed out of what looked like a hole from the outside and it was under a bush even at that.

"Now you must remember, if at any time you want to come to visit. Anyone can open this door just by pulling up and back on it, but all the other doors must have the right combination of stones turned. Start with the stone on the left and turn it once to the left on the next door you turn the second stone on the right and turn it to the right two times. Then on the third door you turn the third stone on the left to the left three times and so on. When you get to the last door there will be no stones to turn and all you do there is give the door a quick push and back up fast, it will open far enough for you to grab the hand grip and open it the rest of the way." she explained.

We gave her hugs and waved goodbye as we walked down the hills toward camp.

As we got into sight of camp Strong Bow saw us and shouted back to the others as he ran out to meet us.

"I found the message you left at the opening of the cave. But I couldn't find you. We thought you had been picked up or were laying hurt somewhere." he said.

"If that had happened, one of us would have sent a message somehow." I said giving everyone there hugs and then smiled at Notnah (Not).

"You would not believe the things that we saw today and the places we've been." Notnah (Not) and I looking at each other and started laughing.

"Well, we all want to hear about it after we eat. It sounds like a good campfire tale." said Strong Bow.

On our way back to camp I thought I saw something out of the corner of my eye. So I turned to take a better look and I spotted Starneah (Star) sneaking through the bushes ever so quietly. I looked at Notnah (Not), winked and tipped my head, and we both let out another laugh.

After everyone had eaten that evening we all sat down around the fire and it was Notnah (Not) and my turn to tell about the city we had found and the people we had a chance to meet. Well, needless to say, the whole story sounded so outrageous

that it was really hard to believe then
Notnah (Not) and I got the idea to call out
Starneah (Star) who had been hiding all this
time listening to all the other stories.

Everyone's eyes grow large when
little Starneah (Star) came walking out of the
bushes from behind Notnah (Not) and
climbed onto the rock beside him and
wrapped her tail around his arm.

"So this is Starneah (Star)? She is
quite cute for being a little short person."
said Strong Bow with a wink to me.

"With all that has happened, I think
it has been a long day for all of us and it is
time to go to bed." Two Wolves said.

"Yes amacron (morning) will come
early." chimed in Healing Waters.

"Starneah (Star) can sleep with us
tonight." said Strong Bow putting his hand
out to Starneah (Star). She took his hand
and grabbed mine with her free hand and
we all strolled off to our sleeping areas.

The sun was just starting to give its
first amacron (morning) rays when we were
all awakened by this loud screeching and
barking type wails. I got to my feet with
Starneah (Star) holding on to one arm.

*"It is my people, I left yesterday without
letting anyone know where I was going."* she
said hanging her head and her tail drooped
around her feet.

"Okay then we will both go out and you can tell them what happened and why you left without telling anyone." I said opening the tent flap.

With a short yelp and a few clicks, Starneah (Star) had the attention of their hunting party.

As she continued to make a few noises now and then you could tell she was telling them what happened and some of the stories she had overheard and why she didn't have time to tell anyone where she was going. I knew Notnah (Not) and I was able to understand what was being said because we had gotten connected to these people while we were with them below.

I looked over at Two Wolves and smiled to let him know it was going well, but he just smiled back and nodded at me toward Starneah (Star). Then the thought hit me that she somehow had turned this conversation into a public one and that most if not all of us could understand what was being said. I breathed a sigh of relief when I thought of all the explaining I wouldn't have to do.

After Starneah (Star) had explained everything and they started to leave, Healing Waters stepped forward and handed them a few good size baskets of fresh berries that had been picked the evening before.

They took them and with a smile Starneah (Star) waved. *"May our peoples always be like family and one at peace with each other."*

With them headed back to their home, I got to thinking. "You know, Strong Bow, I wonder if when we get back to Cyterrious, if we could find a trace of the peoples that Starneah (Star) and her people came to Earth with?" I said looking up at the sky.

"I'm not sure but I will help if that is what you want to do." he said while giving me a hug.

"I think it might be neat to meet the people now and let them know we had found what was left of the landing party." I said smiling at him.

"But if memory serves, you told us that Arnic (Arnold) was from Debon 4 of the Stanic system, isn't that right?" he questioned.

"Yes, that's right, and....?" I asked looking back at him while we walked to the hill at the edge of camp to watch the stars for a while.

"Well, I remember reading something about one of their stars going nova a while back." he said.

"I'm glad that it is a clear night. The stars are so pretty." I said with a sigh after sitting for a few keptrons (minutes).

"Morning will come early so we can't sit here long." Strong Bow reminded me.

"Okay" I said getting up and heading back to camp to get some sleep.

Chapter Fourteen
Close Call

Papa Two Wolves spotted us as we were strolling out to where the group was planting the herbs

"Hey you two, stop that messing around and help us get the rest of these plants planted before time gets away." playfully scolded Two Wolves with a laugh.

"Well, I guess we can help if it is needed." we said almost at the same time, as we started laughing.

I walked over to where Healing Waters and some of the other women were getting ready to plant a flat of seedlings. I got there just in time to make sure that these plants were planted in the right place. Strong Bow headed for the group of older plants still on their flats waiting to be planted

"This type of plant needs shade most of the time, so if we plant them in between those trees, over there, they should be okay."

I said, as I pointed to a small grove of trees not too far away.

"Elaytay (Tay)! Which plants get planted near the water?" yelled Strong Bow from across the way.

"The two flats to the right of your feet." I yelled back while pointing.

After a while we had all of the plants planted and all of the watering ditches dug.

The clouds where gathering for what may become and good rain.

Two Wolves noticing the clouds, said, "Looks like we will get a chance to see how well our watering ditches hold up." pointing at the clouds.

"Hey everyone, we will have to hurry if we are going to beat the rain storm that looks to be headed our way." I shouted pointing toward the sky. The heavier clouds were building fast. It looked like we were in for a good size storm.

It rained for the rest of the day and into the night. Getting up the next amacron (morning), we were all in a hurry to see what had happened with the plants we had planted the day before.

At first glance, I could see we were going to have some improving to do. Some of our watering ditches had gotten to full and the sides had worn down and if we didn't get started it wouldn't get finished today.

"Ok, we have our work cut out for us today. But I think we can get it done in about half a sestron (day), if about ten of us work hard." I said, looking at everyone standing nearby. "So if everyone that isn't helping in the fields can help by supplying the rest of us with food and water, we can keep at this till it is finished." I continued.

Healing Water got most of the women and headed back to camp. They were going to help in their own way.

"We are going to need the tools we used yesterday and something to haul flat river stones in." I sort of yelled, trying to make sure everyone knew what was needed.

Gathering a small team of the young brave, Tall Grass, headed for the river to gather the flat stones we were going to need.

Running Elk was last seen running for camp, soon returned with a travois to help haul the stones from the riverbed.

"Good idea Running Elk." I said.

"Yes, good thinking." Chimed Two Wolves as Running Elk kept running toward the river, with a few children running alongside him.

We were all working on the ditches, trying to get them reinforced in a way that they would hold their shapes no matter how much water came into them.

With a scream, everyone stopped what they were doing.

"It came from the river." shouted Two Wolves.

Everyone took off running for the river. When we got there we found out that one of the children, Snow Robin, had pick up a rock where a snake had been hiding and had gotten bit.

"Did anyone see the snake? Do we know what kind of snake it was, we need to know." I questioned, while Strong Bow ran back to camp for the snake medical kit we had brought.

"I didn't see the whole snake but the back half I saw was black with light yellow stripes going down its body, all the way to its tail and it went that way" said Red Fox while I put my headband on tight above the bite on her arm.

"Good, that is a relief," said Elmosa (Wolf).

"Why is that?" questioned Red Fox.

"Because the dark snake that have the light colored stripe going long ways down their body are not poisonous. At least all of them I have been reading about." he said.

"That is good, then the only thing we will have to watch for is infection from the teeth of the snake, and that will show up as a high fever." I said.

Strong Bow came running back with the kit. "Here is the kit. What kind of snake was it?" he asked.

"According to the information that Red Fox gave me, it was from the Colubridae family of snakes. So all we need is the antiseptic, a clean wrap and some tape for the bitten area." I said.

"Tape?" questioned Two Wolves.

"Yes, here take a piece." I said sticking a piece to his hand with a smile. "I figured that is the easiest way to let you know what it is." I added as we all laughed.

"This stuff you call tape is very strange. It is like getting honey on a piece of cloth." he said laughing.

"Well they are sort of the same, they will both come off in water," I said looking over at Two Wolves. "So you keep this dry for the next day of so." I said turning my attention back to Snow Robin.

"Ok," she said as she got up and headed towards camp with Red Fox beside her.

They headed back to camp and the rest of us went back to fixing the water ditches.

Soon we had all the turns in our water ditches reinforced with the stone.

"Good job everyone! Now when a lot of water runs through the ditches, they won't give way to the force so easily." I said giving everyone a smile, and with that everyone gave out with their happy yelps.

Notnah (Not) was celebrating the help he had given, by stomping his feet and sort of dancing in a small circle.

Chapter Fifteen
Cause For Celebration

Later on that evening after dinner and during story telling time, one of the Elders stood up and said he had an announcement to make to everyone.

Looking over at Rogna (Rodger), Elder Dancing Beaver said, "With all that has happened since Strong Bow and his family have gotten here, with the planting of healing plants, the great hunt, and the meeting of a new peoples living nearby...I want you to meet someone who comes to us with great backing in regards to the kind of person he is, and he has passed our tribal tests. I want everyone to welcome Rogna (Rodger) to our tribe, who will from this day forward be known as Soaring Hawk. I also understand that he has asked for Morning Star's hand in marriage." looking back at Morning Star, and Running Bear, who nodded at him, "Which has just been accepted." he continued. "So this means the next 4 day will be celebration while all the arrangements are being made for the new couple. And with that I say good night to all." as he turns and left the story circle.

It was getting late, so the fire was watched by a few and the rest of us went to bed.

Early next amacron (morning) the whole camp was buzzing about the newest member of their tribe, Soaring Hawk and his joining to Morning Star. There were the preparations to be made for a new tent and the wedding clothes, the foods and dried fruits and feastings that would go on until the wedding and after that until the couple came back from their first few days together.

I knew we would have to be leaving soon and was in hopes that we could stay until they got married.

"I talked to Norzalon (Red) over the transmitter earlier today to find out how long we had before the planet would force us to leave." I explained that to Strong Bow later that evening.

"So what was the answer? How long do we have, will we get to stay till they get married?" he asked.

"Yes but then we have to leave in 24 decons (hours) after that, because of the openings." I said.

"I will explain all this to the boys tomorrow, and also to the counsel and see if we can speed things up just a little." he said.

Time went by fast and it came time for Soaring Hawk and Morning Star to get married. Everything couldn't have gone better. It was perfect and really beautiful. I managed to get a little of it on the videe holled so we could watch it later on...and no one knew I got it.

After the wedding, we all went and said our goodbyes and told them we thought we could come back sometime, but wasn't sure when.

The amacron (morning) after they had left for their few sestrons (days) together, Norzalon (Red) and the crew landed to pick us up for our trip back home.

"Strong Bow, I want to go with you back to your home. Can I please? I don't have anything here and nothing to take with me, and maybe I can help in some way. I love to learn and explore. Please." Notnah (Not) begged.

"I will have to ask, I will have to talk to Norzalon (Red) our Captain and to Elaytay (Tay) and the others. I will let you know. Okay?" said Strong Bow.

Strong Bow found me gathering up our gear and the few things I wanted to take back. I had just got Zigmo put back in the cage and latched the door when he told me what Notnah (Not) had asked.

"Well, have you talked to the Captain and Paleeto (Pal) yet?" I asked.

"No, I wanted to get your idea on the subject first." he said. "It's ok with me." he added.

"I don't mind and I can't think of a good reason why he couldn't come back with us, who knows maybe he can help us find the rest of his people and Starneah (Star)'s too." I said. "How about you helping me carry all these things to the ship and I will ask Paleeto (Pal) and the Captain if it is alright for Notnah (Not) to come back with us." I added.

"Ok!" he said gladly as he started grabbing up all the things nearest him.

Notnah (Not) came running up about halfway back to the ship. *"Did they say? I mean can I come with you?"* he asked excitedly.

"We haven't had a chance to ask yet. We are on our to the ship now, come with us." I said.

Notnah (Not) took a few things from Strong Bow and ran out ahead of us, to the ship.

Excitedly he waited for us to catch up
with him, but he did, and managed to stand
pretty still while waiting.

Norzalon (Red) was just coming out
of the ship to look for me. "Oh Good your
here, I was just going over the supplies we
have on hand and this is the list of the things
we need. Maybe you can find them for us."
he said handing me the list.

"Yes Sir, not a problem," I said quickly
looking over the list.

He turned to walk back into the ship.

"Captain Norzalon (Red), I have a
request." I said quickly, before he got out of
ear shot.

"Yes, and what is that?" he said as
turned around and noticed Notnah (Not)
swaying ever so slightly. "But first, who is
this fine fellow?" he added with a smile.

Notnah (Not) smiled back in his own
little odd way.

"Sir, this is Notnah (Not), I have found
him to be very helpful during our stay here."
I explained. "He is a young teen sasquatch,
who's parentless due to the X men."

Captain Norzalon (Red), looked at
me a little odd.

"You remember sir, the little short
gray guys with the big black eyes." I said.

"Oh yes, please continue." he said.

"Sir! Notnah (Not) here, wants permission to travel back to Cyterrious with us and become part of our team." A sort of requested.

"Well," Norzalon (Red) said stroking his chin. "I think we can manage the room and the weight since we don't have any plants to take back with us." he said with a smile.

Notnah (Not) was almost jumping with joy at hearing this and was saluting the captain with both hands, first with one hand and then the other. I reached over and grabbed his hands, "It's OK Notnah (Not), a one hand salute is plenty and only once." I said. At this point he gave Norzalon (Red) a deep bow. With this Strong Bow and I had to give a slight chuckle.

"He must have seen Elmosa (Wolf), Mozla (Jeff) and Rogna (Rodger) playing around earlier today." I explained.

"I think all that was a thank you." I explained to Norzalon (Red).

"But! You will have to take classes and pass them and go through ship and mission training when you get to Cyterrious. You understand this, right?"

Norzalon (Red) asked, trying to look stern. Notnah (Not) nodded his head so fast that his hair was flouncing around wildly.

"I believe that is a Yes." I said with a smile

Notnah (Not), stooped over slowly and picked up the bundles he had placed on the ground. Looked at the three of us and gave a big smile, and with that we followed Norzalon (Red) onto the ship.

Chapter Sixteen
Finding an Oztinsizer

Notnah (Not) spotted Paleeto (Pal) and gave out a loud squeal.

"It's OK Notnah (Not)." I said grabbing Notnah (Not) by the arm. *"This is our friend Paleeto (Pal). He is Not part of the group that took your parents. Paleeto (Pal) is a completely different race, from a different planet."* I explained trying to calm Notnah (Not) down. *"Now slow down your breathing."* I continued.

Paleeto (Pal), knew what Notnah (Not) was thinking and chimed in. *"You see, Notnah (Not), I am not the same as the ones that took your parents. I know what you are thinking and can talk to you in the same way as your parents did. In fact your people's home planet is in the same area of space as my own."*

"Paleeto (Pal), why don't you show Notnah (Not) around the ship and show him where he will be sleeping, while I get our things squared away and go fill this list." I said while holding up the list.

"That is a great idea." Paleeto (Pal) said while motioning for Notnah (Not) to follow him.

After getting all our things put away, I went out to gather all the things that Captain Norzalon (Red) had written on the list.

I looked at the list again as I walked out the ship door and down the ramp and I noticed that some of these thing, I didn't remember seeing in or around camp.

"Papa Two Wolves, I think I will need your help!" I yelled to get Two Wolves's attention.

"Elaytay (Tay), what will you need my help with? I will always help if I can, you know that." he said.

"Well, this is a list of the things that Captain Norzalon (Red) says we need for the trip home. I will read them off to you." I suggested as I started naming some of the things on the list..

"Right off the start, I would have to say, I don't think we have this, thing you call a Os-tin-sizer, I have never heard of one. What is it" he asked, looking curious.

"Well it is hard to explain, knowing that you don't have one is enough, but to give you a little information about it. It helps to relax the neck muscles." I said with a smile.

"We have herbs that will help with that, but I would say, check with Starneah

(Star) if you have time. Meanwhile I will gather the herbs, and the rest of the things you named off." he said as he walked off.

"Thank you," I call as I started off for Starneah (Star)'s home.

I was glad it was still fairly early in the day, because going to see Starneah (Star) would take me the larger part of a decon (hour).

Once I found the bush and opened the door, Starneah (Star)'s city seemed a lot longer this time, maybe because I was traveling the trail alone. Finally I got to the first door and Starneah (Star) was waiting for me just outside it.

"You came back to visit?" she asked.

"Well, I came back to see you before I leave to go back to my home on Cyterrious, and also to ask if you have an item that our Captain says he needs for the trip home." I said.

"And what is that." she asked.

"It is an item that Arnic (Arnold) may have used from time to time. It goes around the back of the neck and relaxes the muscles. We call it an oztinsizer." I tried explaining.

"I don't remember the name but I think I remember seeing pictures of something around his neck. Maybe it would be with all his things in the galleo room. We will go see, Follow me." she said as she scurried down the passageway with me right behind her.

She was running so fast that her tail was trailing behind her and it was hard not to step on it.

Then we were there, standing in front of this large wooden door that looked like it should have been in a castle. *"It's in there."* she said, *"But none of us have ever been strong enough to open the door."* she said, looking up at its size.

"Let me see if I can open it. You mean none of your people have ever seen what is inside this room?" I said while pulling on the door's locking bolt.

All of a sudden it gave way with a thump and a clank. I found myself on the floor. By this time there was a group of Starneah (Star)'s people waiting to see what was hidden in this room. As I pulled the very large door open, the group's eyes grew very large.

In this room, there was a large soft bed in one corner, a large table nearby full of all sorts of shiny objects, some old maps, a chest full of armor and a space helmet in one corner, there were some bells, a stringed half full of animal teeth and some sort of horn. Over the end of the bed hung a large worn out furry looking object.

Starneah (Star) and her people were having fun with the shiny plates, cups and the bells.

"Starneah (Star)!, I think this is what I was looking for." I said as I picked it up. *It felt like a scatna purring in my hand. I put it around my neck and it felt real good. "Yes, I think this is what Captain Norzalon (Red) was talking about. May I take this with me?"* I asked.

Starneah (Star) looked at one of their elders, then back at me. *"Yes Lapan (Pan) says it is the least we can do since you opened this room for us."* she relayed with a smile.

"I must leave, please tell you people I said Thank you and if it is ok with them, maybe I can come back sometime and see them again." I said as I turned to walk out of the room.

Starneah (Star) caught up with me in the passageway and said *"It is ok with them, you and your family can come and visit anytime. I will walk with you to the top."*

"Don't get in trouble this time." I said with a smile.

"I have permission this time" she said.

The distance seemed short as we talked all the way to the top. She wanted to know about my planet and if we could find her people's planet, maybe we could send word that they are doing fine.

I said goodbye and left her standing by the bush, waving at me.

It didn't take long after that to get back to camp, and Two Wolves caught up with me right off. He was carrying a large bundle.

"Well here are the things you were asking for earlier." he said.

"Thank you," I said while taking the bundle and giving him a hug. "We will be leaving in a little over a decon (hour), can you gather everyone together?" I asked.

"Yes I will, but what about Rogna (Rodger) and Morning Star?" he asked.

"Strong Bow, the boys and I all said our goodbyes before they left camp for their life together." I informed him with a smile.

"That is good, yes I will tell the others." he said.

I took in one last check of the camp before going back to the ship and on the way, I let Mozla (Jeff) and Elmosa (Wolf) know it was time to be leaving.

Chapter Seventeen
Blasting off

"Good you are back, and it looks like you have everything I asked for, including the Oztinsizer. I didn't think you would be able to find one of these. Wow this is one of the better ones too." Norzalon (Red) said examining it up close. "So now, you have to tell me where you got this." he questioned.

"We had a chance to meet some of the people that got here while the large animals roamed this planet and they learned to live underground." I said.

"So who are these people? he asked.

"I don't know that much about them, except that the main people that looked like us died a long while ago. I don't know maybe you have heard for their Captain in history. A Captain Arnic (Arnold)? I said.

"Arnic (Arnold)?, humm, Arnic (Arnold). Yes seems to me that there was some talk about a group that went off on their own and just disappeared and no one ever heard from them again and if memory serves, Arnic (Arnold) was that Captain's name. So they landed here and I get to use his

Oztinsizer." he said with a belly laugh on his way back into the ship.

"Where are the boys?" asked Strong Bow.

"They are coming, I saw them on my way back to the ship. They will be here soon and so will everyone who wants to say goodbye." I reassured him.

"Good, here they are now." he said.

The boys came running up the ramp and into the ship.

"Slow down now. Get all your things ready for lift off." I instructed them.

"Ok mom," Elmosa (Wolf) said on his way past me.

"Yes ma'am," Mozla (Jeff) said with a salute and a giggle.

"Those two, sometimes I wonder." I said looking at Strong Bow and shaking my head. "No wonder Notnah (Not) gets mixed up watching them." I said laughing.

"Fun should be children's middle names." Strong Bow said with a grin.

"You know I think you are right.". Paleeto (Pal) agreed as he came out onto the ramp, *"We have to leave in thirty keptrons (minutes). I hope you friends come soon the say their goodbyes."* he added.

Just then Strong Bow spotted what seemed to be the whole tribe coming up the path. A few of them were carrying small gifts.

"I am glad they aren't carrying anything large, we might have had to leave them here since we are taking Notnah (Not)." I said laughing.

As they all gathers in close to the ship, Strong Bow stepped forward. "Here we are again, standing on the ramp of the ship that is to carry us away., I am not sure when we will be back again, but if time carries us like I want it to, we will see you in about another ten to thirteen sectos (years)." he announced. "Be good and take good care to each other and may happiness be with all of you. We love you. Now there is just enough time for hugs all round, then you must back away from the ship so you don't get hurt." he said as we walked down the ramp to give each one hugs and love pats.

"Now all of you back up into those trees so we know you are safe from the lift off." Strong Bow and I said together with a wave from the ship's door.

Paleeto (Pal) stepped into the doorway so he could wave at the people that remembered him from his first visit.

After setting the prox sensors, we went in a sat down in our seats and strapped in. We could see that everyone was clear of the ship.

"Prepare for blast off" Captain Norzalon (Red) announced.

"Yes sir, clear and set, firing Sir" I shouted for all to hear. Notnah (Not), Elmosa (Wolf) and Mozla (Jeff) were in one of the side rooms, laughing. That was a good sound as we took off.

"Out of gravity's pull and setting controls for home at top speed. Sir" I said.

Getting out of my seat I could see that the boys and Notnah (Not) were playing on Elmosa (Wolf)'s bed with Zigmo. "You boys be careful with Zigmo, she is young and you don't want her turning mean, so don't tease her." I warned.

Strong Bow and I had other duties we had to attend to in the first and last part of the trip. After we were completely under way we had time to visit and complete some of the projects we were bringing back with us. We would be landing on Cyterrious in a few mistrons (months).

Time passed quickly, and as we got closer to Cyterrious, Norzalon (Red) got an update on our sciences. "We just got a message from Science Central and it seems that we have made a few breakthroughs in time travel." he announced.

"Now that sounds real interesting. I want to check that out when we get home." I said looking at Strong Bow with a big grin. I loved science and exploration of all kinds. I knew I want to be involved in it somehow.

"Yes, I guess you will. I know that is your 2nd love above family. So I say look into it and see what it's about." Strong Bow said, giving his approval.

Time passed quickly and the boys taught Notnah (Not) all they could about our planet in the short time they had. One of the last things they showed him was a picture of the planet up close.

"Oh!, you didn't tell me that your sky was purple and that the tree tops all grew together." Notnah (Not) said with his eyes very wide. "I will have to get used to seeing a purple sky. I like blue skies." he said.

"Well this is just one of the changes to get used to." Elmosa (Wolf) said. "But most of the people there can talk to you like we do."

"We mean in your head." said Mozla (Jeff) with a chuckle.

"Ok guys, it is time to buckle in. We will be landing shortly." I said.

Paleeto (Pal) announced. *"Everyone buckle up we are starting the landing count down now."*

"Sir! Contact has been made with Communication Central, and we have the go ahead to land, but they are saying there is a bad storm in the area we were to land in. So they have changed our landing site. Sir! They have changed it to Old Ridge Camp near the base of Pastida. Sir!" I said, addressing Captain Norzalon (Red).

"Thank you, Elaytay (Tay)." came his reply.

"Paleeto (Pal)! Ready for you to correct our course for landing at the Old Ridge Camp near the base of Pastida." said Captain Norzalon (Red).

"Sir! New course data has been entered and the corrections have been made. We will be landing in 10 keptrons (minutes). Sir!" said Paleeto (Pal).

"Sir! Transports will be waiting our arrival, Sir!" I announced.

"Touch Down, at last." said Paleeto (Pal).

"It is going to be so great getting home, I can hardly wait. I have missed Kerzna (Kern). I think you will like him." said Elmosa (Wolf) looking over at Notnah (Not).

"Who is Kerzna (Kern)?" said Notnah (Not).

"You mean what is Kerzna (Kern)." chimed in Mozla (Jeff).

"Only the best friend and pet there is." said Elmosa (Wolf) proudly.

"I think there is a lot more to learn about your planet than you have showed me on the way here." said Notnah (Not).

"You will like it here, I am sure of that." reassured Elmosa (Wolf).

"You can stay with us and the boys can help you learn more." I said.

"Gather up all you things, boys. We are going home." said Strong Bow.

Chapter Eighteen
Home At Last

We loaded all of our bundles, the ship's crew, our whole family including Notnah (Not) into the shuttle and headed back to Communication Central.

After arriving, we took the time to record all of the date from our missions and leave the samples we had gathered while on planet Earth.

I had set a message ahead, telling them about Notnah (Not) and got a message back saying to tell him welcome, and got a return message. Grams said she would join the boys in teaching him the basics of surviving on our world in society. I agreed that would be a great idea.

About the time I had finished my part at Communication Central, I figured that Gramps and Grams would be arriving to pick all of us up.

And as I came out of the last office, I spotted Gramps coming through the front doors.

"Gramps, I am glad to be back. We had a great visit and brought back gifts from our other family," I said with a big smile, while reaching out to give him a big hug.

Just then Strong Bow walked up. "Hi Gramps," he said give Gramps a hug, "Where is Grams," he asked. Just then she came walking through the doors.

"We were wondering where you were. Strong Bow had just asked about you," I said giving her a huge hug.

"So I have two questions," she said while looking around. "Where is Rogna (Rodger)? And where is the Notnah (Not) fellow you mentioned?" she asked.

"Ok, to start with, you remember we talked about Strong Bow using his family and camp on Earth as a template for the creation dome camping trips? And I'm sure I mentioned that Rogan liked Morning Star, Strong Bow's little sister?" I asked.

"Yes," Grams answered slowly. "What happened?" she asked looking over at Strong Bow and raising one eye brow at him.

Strong Bow started laughing, "Nothing bad Grams. He found out that Morning Star was a real person and that she was just like the one in the creation dome. Well, they fell in love, he joined the tribe and they got married. They decided to stay on Earth."

"Oh my," said Grams as she started to laugh. Then she caught a glimpse of Notnah (Not). "And this must be the strong good looking fellow called Notnah (Not), you told me about?" she said looking at him with a smile.

Elmosa (Wolf) just rounded a corner of a nearby hall. "Hi Granma, I see you have met Notnah (Not). We met him while we were with Dad's family. The x-men took his parents, so we brought him home with us. I missed you and Granma. How is Kerzna (Kern) doing?" he asked giving grandpa a big hug.

"He is doing good. I have been keeping him busy with some of the neighborhood kids. I told him you were on your way back and he was very happy to hear that." Gramps said returning the hug and giving him a pat on the back. *"Well Notnah (Not), you will have to tell us all about yourself and your people. Do you know or remember many of the stories that your parents told you."* Grams asked on our way to their shuttle.

We gathered up what we had brought back with us and all walked together to the shuttle and soon we were all on our way back home

"Mozla (Jeff), how are you doing son? You have been real quiet since you got back," asked Gramps.

"Ok, I guess, It is just sort of hitting me now that Rogna (Rodger) didn't come back with us. He is an old married man now. That is just hard to believe," Mozla (Jeff) said.

"Well, not quite an OLD married man," said Strong Bow jokingly while nudging him a little. "Cheer up. I left them a present before we left," he continued.

"What did you leave them, dad?" asked Elmosa (Wolf) excitedly.

"Yeah, you brought it up now you have to tell," I added wanting to know too.

"Well," Strong Bow said clearing his voice and stalling a little.

"Come on out with it, tell us we are all waiting with open ears," said Mozla (Jeff).

"I left them with the best communication set up Captain Norzalon (Red) had on board that he could turn loose of. Rogna (Rodger) and Morning Star can send us a message and we will get it in two pestrons (weeks). That is the turnaround time it takes for our messages to travel that distance. That is a lot faster than when Elaytay (Tay) first landed on Earth." Strong Bow said with a very large smile.

"Yea! All Right!, we can talk to Rogna (Rodger) and Morning Star when we want to," shouted the boys almost in harmony.

"Well I guess you just made their day," I said giving Strong Bow a big hug.

"I am glad to know that we will be able to know they are ok and what all they are doing once in a while," said Grams while glancing away from the road.

"The storm is getting worse, but not to worry, we will all be home soon," said Gramps as we rounded the last curve. We drove up the driveway, as we got out of the shuttle, we gathered up everything we needed that night. Just before going into the house, the door blew open on the barn, and we all heard Kerzna (Kern) squeal in fear.

He didn't know that we had just got back. He thought he was all alone and the storm was going to carry him away.

Notnah (Not)'s, thoughts rang out over the howling winds. *He is afraid of the storm, I can hear him but I don't think he can understand me.* he said holding his ears. His long fur was whipping back and forth with the changing winds.

"Yes, Notnah (Not), you help Grams and Elaytay (Tay) get everything into the house before it all gets wet. Strong Bow, the Boys and I will attend to Kerzna (Kern),"

Gramps yelled over the whipping winds and the thundering rain.

We got everything into the house and soon after, the back door opened and while Strong Bow worked hard at holding the door steady, the boys and Gramps coaxed Kerzna (Kern) into the house. Grams walked into the kitchen in time to see what was going on and started laughing. At that point Kerzna (Kern) came in willingly. Then came the timid question, *"It is ok, Grams for me to be inside this nestron (night)?"* ask Kerzna (Kern).

"Yes, my fuzzy friend, it is fine for you to be with us this nestron (tonight)," Grams answered with a large grin.

At that point Kerzna (Kern) noticed that Elmosa (Wolf) was home, and you could see his eyes light up with happiness. *"You are home Elmosa (Wolf). I have missed you. Gramps has tried to keep me busy working with the young ones that live close by this house. But I still missed having our camping trips and our long hikes,"* he said looking straight into Elmosa (Wolf)'s eyes.

Elmosa (Wolf) had a small tear trying to sneak out of the corner of his eyes when he gave Kerzna (Kern) a hugh hug and said, "I missed you too you big fuzzy guy."

Kerzna (Kern) caught sight of Notnah (Not) just then and backed up rather quickly tuning the kitchen table on end. "Hold on

Kerzna (Kern)," said Elmosa (Wolf) in a very calm voice. "This is Notnah (Not), he is a friend. His family was on Earth, he is now alone, so he is staying here with all of us now."

Kerzna (Kern) settled and Notnah (Not) walked the rest of the way into the room.

"Hello Kerzna (Kern), sorry if I frightened you. I must look odd to you." said Notnah (Not). *"I would like to know more about your people and the things you know and have learned while you have been here. I have so many questions."* he continued.

"Not to nestron (night). There will be plenty of time for questions and adventures later. It is time for all of us to get some rest and that means you two also," said Grams looking straight at Notnah (Not) and Kerzna (Kern). "Now I will bring you blankets and pillows for tonight and there is a bed upstairs if you want to sleep in one Notnah (Not) or you can sleep down here. But there will be no talking, is that clear." Grams said sternly.

"Ok, we understand," said both Notnah (Not) and Kerzna (Kern) almost at the same time. *"I will sleep here with Kerzna (Kern) if you don't mind Grams,"* said Notnah (Not).

"That is fine, but no talking to nestron (night)," she said again to get the point across. Both Notnah (Not) and Kerzna (Kern) looked at each other giving Grams a grin in their own ways and nodded. "And the rest of you, go get in your beds, the lights will be going off in a few keptrons (minutes). Grams announced.

Everyone knew they had better hurry, because when Grams said anything in that matter of fact tone, you knew she meant business. And that what she said was the only warning you were going to get. So we all said "Good Nestron (night)" and got in our beds. Within a few keptrons (minutes) all of the lights were off, except for a small low light she left on for Kerzna (Kern).

Strong Bow and I lay in the bed and listened to the stormy winds wailing outside and the shadows of the trees swept back and forth across the window. We finally fell asleep. With amacron (morning) came the most beautiful purple skies I had ever remembered. Had I really missed the purple skies that much?

"It is good to be back home again. I have almost forgotten how beautiful the purple skies could be," I said as Strong Bow and I walked into the kitchen just in time to hear Grams.

Chapter Nineteen
Those Poor Chickens

"Ok you two, time to get up and go outside, check out Kerzna (Kern)'s barn and see what all needs to be done to it while I make breakfast," She said as she waved both hands in the air to shoo Notnah (Not) and Kerzna (Kern) out the back door.

They both slowly walked out to the barn to see what the damages were from the storm.

Grams turned her attention toward making breakfast for everyone.

Gramps came in to the kitchen about that time and he looked at us and winked. That let me and Strong Bow know he was in a fun mood this sestron (day).

"So Grams what would you think about letting Kerzna (Kern) sleeping in the house every nestron (night)?" he started off the conversation while giving her a quick kiss and a hug around her waist.

"Well how would you like sleeping in the barn?" she asking, while turning her head where he couldn't see her grinning.

It seemed that they both woke up in a playful mood It looked like a fun sestron (day) all round. That is till a squeal came from the direction of the barn.

"*Dead, they died,*" is all we caught, But we couldn't tell whether it was Kerzna (Kern) or Notnah (Not) that was talking. Grams and Gramps both ran for the back yard with us on their heels. Gramps headed for the barn. He came back soon and said, "It was the chickens that died, it seems we lost over half of them in the storm last nestron (night). Kerzna (Kern) was upset because they were his friends or pets or something. I'm not real sure what they would be to him, but he cared about them and is sad over the loss." Gramps informed us.

"Well, gather them up and I will dress them out for dinner," Grams said. "Just get Notnah (Not) and Kerzna (Kern) out of the barn before you gather them up." she continued.

Notnah (Not) is a vegetarian right?" she asked looking at Strong Bow and me.

"Yes as far as we know. I don't ever remember him eating meat except for fish. He likes fish," I answered.

"Good, Gramps is, having them go fishing. They can take Mozla (Jeff) and Elmosa (Wolf) with them," Grams said.

Grams delivered the message to Kerzna (Kern) and Notnah (Not) and I went and woke up the boys. I told them that Notnah (Not) and Kerzna (Kern) were going fishing and may need their help. At hearing that they went running down the stairs and almost made it to the back door before Grams yelled.

"STOP! Neither of you have eaten breakfast yet much less said good sestron (day) to anyone yet. Please don't tell me you forgot your manners on Earth. We may have to send you back to gather them up." she said laughing. "Now sit down and eat first, outside will wait till you get through," she added.

Gramps came back in about that time. "Ok everything you kids will need for fishing is leaning up against the wall of the barn. I just gave Kerzna (Kern) and Notnah (Not) a couple of large bowl of fruit to munch on for breakfast." he said.

Mozla (Jeff) and Elmosa (Wolf) quickly finished eating, gave quick hugs and ran out the door on their way to a new adventure.

The rest of us sat down to a peaceful breakfast and soon after Gramps went out to gather the chickens that died in the storm. Soon he came back in with five dirty chickens and a large grin on his face. Grams and I looked at each other and started laughing.

Grams finally stopped long enough to ask. "What happened to those poor chicken," as Gramps handed them to her.

"It seems that while we were all eating breakfast, Kerzna (Kern) and Notnah (Not) had a burial service for the chickens," he answered while trying to stop laughing.

"I hope you put the mounds back like they were," I said while still laughing. "Because we don't want them to know the chickens are gone." I added.

"True enough, yes I made sure that the graves looked just like they did before I took the chickens out of their graves." Gramps said and then laughed even harder. "Those two take the cake." he said.

"It is going to take some major cleaning to get all the dirt off these chickens, but I can do it," laughed Grams.

"Oh, while you are taking care of things here I want to go check out the new time facility I heard we have now. Do you two know anything about it?" I asked looking at Gramps and Grams.

"We only heard a little about it, but haven't had time to go check it out. I bet that Enah 2 (E 2) would know if anyone does," they said at almost the same time.

"Then I think I will go visit my old friend and see what he knows. Time travel sounds real interesting to me." I said as I gathered the few things I had to take with me. I gave Strong Bow a hug and a loving kiss before leaving.

"Well I guess that leaves us to fix the barn," I heard Strong Bow say as I walked down the steps.

"Yep! Looks like it," Came Gramps reply with a chuckle.

It wasn't far to Enah2 (E2)'s house. I sped up my pace so I could get there before it got any warmer out. There were very few clouds, which meant it was going to be a very warm sestron (day).

I got to Enah 2 (E 2)'s door and rang the bell, but no one answered the door. So I knocked loudly, waited for a few keptrons (minutes) and knocked again.

Just then one of the neighbors stuck their head out of the window next door. "He's not home, I seen him leave for the science Center a little while ago.

I thanked them and started for the Science Center.

While walking I wondered how this neighbor knew just where Enah 2 (E 2) was headed. Did he tell everyone where he was going when he left his house? Or What? It didn't take me long to get to the Science Center and soon found Enah 2 (E 2).

He spotted me just as I walked into the room. "Elaytay (Tay), welcome back! When did you get back?" he asked while walking over to where I was standing.

"Last nestron (night)." I said with a smile.

"You landed during that terrible storm we were having," he asked.

"Yes, that was the worst storm I had ever seen here. Have we had many like that while I was away?" I asked.

"No. Just one other, but this one was worse. We had some major damage from this one along the shoreline on the East side. It took out some of the power units. So what brought you to the science center"? he asked.

"I want to find out more about this time travel project I heard about on my way back home," I said, while looking around. There seems to be a few changes since I was here last," I continued.

"Yes, well you know how science goes. It waits for no one," he said with a chuckle.

"So tell me, are we sending people on time missions now? If so how far back are we going and for how long?" I asked shooting off questions to him like rockets firing.

"Woe, slow down. There is plenty of time to find out," he said with a kind of snicker. "That's funny, you have plenty of time. Get it?" he asked with a big grin.

"Yes I get it and you have gained a sense of humor while I was gone," I said with an inquisitive smile.

"Yes, that was something we sintos have been working on. It helps us to be more like our counter parts." he replied.

"Talking about counter parts, how is Master Enahsto (Professor)?" I asked.

"I am sorry to tell you, but he was in an accident while you were away and didn't make it. The doctors said he was just too old and his heart failed him for the third time and they couldn't fix it," he said looking sort of sad.

"I'm going to miss him, he was a good friend and teacher, he helped me get my first mission," I said with a tear welling up. I had to swallow hard and get my mind on other things to keep from crying.

"I remember all that. You know I do have all of his memories as if they were all mine," Enah 2 (E 2) reminded me.

"Yes, that is right, so then you know how important it is for me to find out all that I can about this new time travel program we have now," I explained.

"Yes, I know. But the new program has a lot of things to learn and it is just now getting off the ground. We are still experimenting with things. We haven't gotten to the point where we are letting humans go out on missions yet," Enah 2 (E 2) explained.

"So is there a place on the team for me? I want to work on the development of the time travel program and devices," I pleaded.

"We will see. I will have to talk to a few people before I can give you an answer. And that may take a while," he said.

"How long are we talking about? I asked rubbing my hands together. "Oh and by the way we brought back a young Sasquatch from Earth," I added.

"Really, maybe I can come by later and meet him. Would that be ok," he suggested.

"Sure I don't see a problem with that. But I do have to let you know that one of us will have to be on hand to translate for you," I replied.

"What do you mean translate?" he asked.

"Well sasquatches are telepathic and they can't hear sinthos talk or think," I explained.

"Oh I am sure he will be able to understand me. I have the newest implant. Would you like to see, oh I mean hear," he said with a laugh.

"Yes," I said feeling a little puzzled.

"So how is this can you hear me ok? What do you think? Pretty cool huh? " he asked, looking pretty proud of himself.

"That is way cool. I love it. That is great. So how were you able to do that?" I asked wanting to know more.

"Well we all got together and studied the human brain and found out that thoughts vibrate at a special rate of speed. So that if we were to put our thoughts through a translator that could translate them to the right vibratory rate then all of you would be able to hear us and we could reverse it so we can hear you too. Does that make since to you?" he asked looking serious at me.

"Yes that makes perfect since to me. I am just wondering why you didn't think of it way before now?" I said with a chuckle. "So when you come over to see Notnah (Not) will you have an answer for me then about the time travel program?" I asked.

"Maybe, I don't know for sure. I have
to meet with the group heads and ask them,
So I don't know if I will have an answer by
then. I want to come and meet, Notnah (Not)?
Is that his name?" he asked

"Yes, Notnah (Not), is his name and
he helped us a lot while we were on Earth.
He learns fast and is a hard worker," I added.
"Ok, I guess I will wait to hear from you then,
but try to make it fast, Ok?" I pleaded.

"As fast as I can. But you know as
well as I do how things work in science
programs," he stressed.

"Ok, Well I guess I will see you at
Grams house later this ponacron (evening)
when you come to meet Notnah (Not)?" I
said verifying the time.

Chapter Twenty
The Zatoth Attack

"It's been great getting back home and seeing you again. Hope you have good news for me soon. See you later," I said as I waved good bye and walked out the big double doors leading me back out under the brilliant purple sky.

On the walk home, I got to thinking about something my dad use to tell me. *"Elaytay (Tay), when you stress about something you want, you are really blocking it from getting to you. So relax, stay calm and keep positive thoughts about how good it will be to get it. But IF for some reason you don't get it at the time you thought you should, then know that there are higher powers that are looking out for you best interest. Let it go and look at you next goal."* My dad was pretty wise. It wasn't very often he didn't get what he wanted at the time he wanted it. So I slowed down my breathing and took a long leisurely walk home, and thought about how great it would be to be able to visit places in the past and see how things really were and not just how the historians thought it may have been. Who knows, we may end up rewriting some of the histories as we know them now. I wonder if our time travel program is taking in other planets too. I hope so. I wonder if there is a way to go into the future and see what may happen. According to all that we know our future isn't written in hard rock as they say, but can change according to shifts in circumstances. Wow what a thought, traveling through time. Well I mean we do a little of that when we travel through space tunnels now, I guess that may be the same. I don't know, but that may be a good question to ask Enah 2 (E 2) when he comes to meet Notnah (Not).

A small bird flew by and the breeze from its wings brought my mind flying back to the here and now. As I neared the edge of town, I could see down into the valley and the colors of the flowers were breath taking. It seems that the whole rainbow had been thrown over it as if it were a large blanket. Some of the flowers still had held tiny small drops of dew on their petals and they glimmered liked as if they had insets of sparkling jewels. Living here on Cyterrious, was sometimes like living in a dream world. The colors on a day like today popped out and grabbed all of your senses at once. I mean the beautiful smells from the flowers, and the colors of them with the back drop of the emerald green forest against the velvety purple skies and then the clear blue streams running through the valley with the luscious green grasses swaying in the cool breezes. I hadn't taken a long walk like this in a very long time. I was surprised at myself. I wasn't in my normal hurried state of mind anymore, I was completely relaxed and enjoying the walk back to the house.

When I reach the house, I was hit with a rush of excitement. Everyone was rushing around as if their world was about to end.

"What is all the excitement about?" I asked as Grams rushed by with her arms full of bandages.

"Notnah (Not), Kerzna (Kern) and the boys went fishing this amacron (morning). None of them thought to take a CAK. Gramps and I forgot that there had been a few escapes from our local PAFOW," she said as she hurried past me.

"Who is hurt and how bad? What animals are loose?" rolled the questions out of my mouth before I even thought, as I scurried down the hall with Grams.

Notnah (Not) lay on the kitchen table with a deep cut across one arm and a long cut on his side. He was squealing as Gramps touched the cut with an antiseptic bandage. "Hold still I need to kill the germs that the Zatoth left in your cuts. I don't want you getting sick and coming down with high fevers," Gramps said.

"Elmosa (Wolf), what happened?" I asked while standing out of the way.

"Mom! It was bad," Elmosa (Wolf) said as he rush to me and hung on to me as if his world was coming to an end.

I wrapped my arms around him and hung on tight. "Now tell me what happened," I said.

"We took everything we thought we needed and went to the lake to go fishing. We had caught a few good size fish when this very large Zatoth ran up and tackled Notnah (Not) from behind, twisted him around and knocked him to the ground. It was all we could do to scare it off. Kerzna (Kern) got up on his back feet and screamed this most ferocious sound. I didn't know that Watapaws could make a noise like that. Well with Mozla (Jeff) and me throwing rock at it. We managed to scare it off. After it left we put Notnah (Not) on Kerzna (Kern)'s back and brought him back here. Kerzna (Kern) is very tall when he stands up. I didn't even know that Watapaw could stand upright," Elmosa (Wolf) explained.

"How bad is it Grams?" I asked.

"Not as bad as it looks," she said with a short smile. "A few more stitches and he will be as good as new after a little rest. But he may have a small scar to show for his fight with a Zatoth."

"There is a group of us that are going out hunting for this Zatoth in about two decons (hours)," Gramps related. "We are going fully armed with CAK and Stunners, this time," he added.

"This time?" I questioned.

"Yes, Well Gramps and a group of the guys went out about a pestron (week) ago. They fired on the Zatoth, but missed him somehow. Gramps said he didn't get a chance to fire before it ran into the heavier wooded areas," explained Grams.

"If that be the case then he will be on the alert this time and harder to find. You aren't planning on staying out overnight are you Gramps?" I asked.

"No, we know better than that. Big Cats like that you don't only hunt when it is light outside," assured Gramps. "OK, Notnah (Not), the bleeding is stopped and you are all sewed up. DO NOT and I mean it do not use this arm. I am tying it up so you can't. Grams is going to take you to the medical center in town and have them take a look at you. I want to make sure I didn't miss anything," Gramps said while helping him to sit up. "Good team work all of you and thank you Kerzna (Kern) for getting him back here," he continued.

"Grams wait up," came a voice from behind me as Mozla (Jeff) and Elmosa (Wolf) ran past me to catch up with Grams and Notnah (Not). "We want to go with you," they said in unison.

I had to chuckle as they ran past. Just then Kerzna (Kern) came up and laid his large head on my shoulder. I reached up and patted him. "Notnah (Not) will be just fine and thanks for all your help," I said.

"*That was all real scary,*" he said with a few odd low rumbles coming from the lower part of his throat.

"Are you trying to learn to talk out loud?" I ask with a smile. Kerzna (Kern) gave me a big grin, showing all his teeth. "And you are learning how to grin," I said with a laugh. "Very good old friend," I said giving him another pat or two and stroked his back.

I poured myself some tea and we went out and sat on the front porch. Kerzna (Kern) sprawled out in one corner where a few of the sun's rays could hit him. We had sat there for a while just enjoying the peace, when about six other guys came walking up the path to the house.

"Hey Boots! Are you ready to go hunting?" one of them shouted from the front steps.

I stood up to get a better look at you was calling out. "Oh sorry, we didn't see you there. We were yelling for your Gramps to hurry up. We want to go get this cat back where it belongs before it hurts someone real bad," one of them explained.

"Boots?" I questioned with a light smile.

"Yeah, well that is a nick name that has stuck with him since school," one of them volunteered with a chuckle.

Gramps came to the door about that time with Strong Bow right behind him. They both were fully armed. I gave Gramps a hug and gave Strong Bow a hug and a kiss.

"Please be careful and stay safe." I said giving Strongbow another kiss.

I sat back down after they were out of sight and almost dosed off when a weird noise caught my attention. It was coming from around back. Kerzna (Kern) heard it to and was on his feet already.

"That is the same rumble I heard just before Notnah (Not) was attacked," he said.

I ran into the house with Kerzna (Kern) on my heels. I grabbed my CAK and we went out the back door after looking through all of the windows on that side of the house.

"Keep your eyes and ears open Kerzna (Kern), we need to know just where this thing is. I don't want either of us getting hurt," I told him.

"*Not to worry, I am listening and watching everything that moves. I think he is around by the trash cans, I am hearing a low rumble from that direction,*" Kerzna (Kern) informed me.

"In that case we don't want to find him waiting around the corner of the house. I am going to walk out away from the house so I can get a better look," I informed Kerzna (Kern).

"*Then I will wait right here next to the corner, just in case he runs towards you, I can jump on him,*" he said.

"Sounds like a good plan," and with that said I started walking out into the yard even with the edge of the house so I wasn't able to see anything around the corner yet. When I got far enough out I stepped into the line of sight and there was the Zatoth tearing into the trash cans. He had ripped two of them to pieces and they were made of metal. Wow that takes force, I thought to myself. About that time he spotted me standing alone in the yard and decided I would make a better meal. He took the first two running steps towards me and I pointed and fired a stun shot that was large enough to knock out a zoobano. The Zatoth fell over with a thud.

"I think he's out," I said.

"*Shoot him again just to make sure,*" Kerzna (Kern) said.

As I stood there with my CAK posed to shoot again if needed, I pushed the button on my side comlink.

"Gramps, Strong Bow? Can you hear me?" I asked, wondering if they were within range.

"Yes, you are coming in clear, what do you need?" asked Gramps.

"Can all of you come back and take this Zatoth to the PAFOW?" I asked.

"What? You have him there?" Gramps asked sounding surprised.

"Yes, but I can't leave him long enough to get anything to tie him up. He is unconscious right now and I have the CAK held on him in case he moves. Kerzna (Kern) want me to shoot him again just in case." I said with a chuckle.

"Ok, we aren't too far away. Hold on we will be there within fifteen keptrons (minutes)," Gramps informed me.

The Zatoth stays out cold, but I was ready to shoot again if needed. Kerzna (Kern) stood right beside me while we waited on everyone to get back.

"Hey Guys! Elaytay (Tay) is around here with the Zatoth," Gramps yelled to the others that had been with him on the hunt. Gramps at this point had his CAK pointed at the Zatoth. Strong Bow had gone after something to tie him up with.

"Good Job honey," he said as he walked up with some of the climbing rope he had brought home with him from Earth. He passed to rope to one of the other guys and gave me a big hug. "How did you manage to get him?" he asked.

I relaxed a little while telling Strong Bow how it all happened and Kerzna (Kern) laid down in the grass beside us.

"The PAFOW keepers will be here soon I just let them know that we had the Zatoth all tied up and ready to be picked up," said one of the guys that was with hunting group.

"Grams just drove into the driveway. I am going to tell her that the Zatoth has been caught, so she doesn't have to worry," I told Strong Bow.

"You got this Gramps?" Strong Bow asked, "Because Grams is home and I want to go see how the hospital trip went. Elaytay (Tay) wait for me," he yelled.

"Sure, go ahead. This Zatoth isn't going anywhere," Gramps answered.

"Grams!" I shouted to get her attention. "The Zatoth has been caught and so all of us are safe now. How did it go at the hospital?" I asked.

"Oh, I was told Gramps did a great job, but he needs to wear bandages for about a pestron (week), and his arm in a slinger tied around his waist. Which he is already complaining about," she said trying not to laugh. "Oh yes, before I forget. Enah 2 (E 2) heard about what happened, don't ask how, because I have no idea. Anyway he said for you to come by the science center in the amacron (morning), he had good news for you," she continued.

"Yeah, that's the words I was waiting for. That means I am going to get to work on the time travel projects," I said almost dancing.

"Wow, you got the answer that quickly. Now that is impressive," Strong Bow said putting his arms around me.

"She said on the way home that this is what she wanted to do when she got home," he said looking at Grams.

Notnah (Not) was out of the shuttle now and both he and the boys were standing next to us.

"Elmosa (Wolf), you and Mozla (Jeff) may want to go see what Gramps is guarding. Your mom here shot it," Strong Bow told Elmosa (Wolf).

"*Is that the thing that made my arm hurt?*" asked Notnah (Not).

"Yes and I shot it for you," I told him hoping that it would make it easier to get him in the house. Strong Bow, Grams and I all got together and sort of nudged Notnah (Not) in the direction of the house. We didn't think he needed to be out there where the Zatoth was.

"Let's all go in the house and have some fruit," Grams said. "Now, that sounds like a good idea, come on Notnah (Not). Let's go have a snack," Strong Bow said sort of pulling Notnah (Not) in the direction of the front door of the house. Notnah (Not) finally gave in and went into the house. We all went to the kitchen and Grams placed bowls of fruit on the table. Kerzna (Kern) was looking through the back door, as if to ask if he could come in and join Notnah (Not).

"Grams, can we let Kerzna (Kern) in for the nestron (night), after all he help me bring down the Zatoth," I asked. "Besides the barn didn't get its door fixed yet," I tried acting like I was begging. Grams started laughing and went over and opened the door for Kerzna (Kern) to come in. "Well I guess this is the way it is supposed to be. All of the family heroes eating together." she laughed.

"But Gramps isn't at the table," I protested.

"Well we have half of our heroes here," she said still laughing. "I am just glad that the zatoth is going back to the PAFOW," she added.

"I can hardly wait till amacron (morning)," I said almost jumping for joy.

"What is happening in the amacron (morning)," Gramps asked while he and the boys walked through the back door.

"I get to start work on the time travel project," I said, trying to hold back my excitement.

"Well in that case, we should all try and get some sleep. Between the storm and the zatoth, we have a lot of clean up and repairs to do starting early," explained Gramps.

"So off to bed for everyone after finishing dinner," he said waving his hands in a shooing motion.

"Ok agreed," I said.

"We are eating light this ponacron (evening)." Grams announced. "We have fruit, wafna bread and cheese." She added.

It didn't take long to eat and it was time for all to get sleep.

"Ok, Good Sleep All," I said with a yawn and Strong Bow and I started up the stairs. We talked for a little while and I drifted off to sleep.

Other Books written
by
Lauresa Tomlinson

Chapter Books

Elaytay (Tay)'s Adventures in Space and Time
Part One – We Came to Visit
Part Three – Time and Time Again

The Turning Stone
My Interview With a Fairy
Magic Under the Pear Tree -
(sort of pt 2 "My Interview With a Fair)
There's an Alien in My Cereal
Secretly Special
Crazy Déjà vu
Crazy Déjà vu –Not Again

Picture Books

Munchie and Goldie – Most Unlikely Friends
Sleepy Time Baby Bear
Cats in Charge

Other

Expressive Tree People (coffee table book)
Studies of Life – Poetry, Love Sonnets &
Thoughts

More Coming Soon
zjavanee@gmail.com